MINISTER'S BRAIN

The most hypnotic villain of all . . .

Get ready for adventure and intrigue.

Prepare to fall under his spell.

Do not try to resist . . .

Are you ready to meet the Demon Headmaster? Here's a taste of what's to come . . .

Suddenly, over on the far side of the room, there was a disturbance.

'No, I *won't*!' shouted a boy's voice. 'I'm sick of being pushed around. I don't like the food and I don't like being shut in. I'm going home.'

Immediately, two men in white coats appeared, one on either side of him. Smoothly they took hold of his arms.

'It is not possible to go home,' said the first man.

'You are to stay here until September the second,' said the other.

Both of them spoke in level voices, with no expression. Exactly the same voices they had used all the time. Dinah found herself shuddering. That was how the prefects at her school used to talk. When the Headmaster was in charge. Coldly. Almost like machines. It was never any use appealing to them or trying to get them to have pity or see sense, because they were not free to soften. They were hypnotized by the Demon Headmaster and under his control. And now these men were the same. She was sure of it. However much the Brains argued with them, they would just go on carrying out their orders.

But the boy who was shouting did not know any of that, of course. He shrieked at the men.

'*I want to go home!*'

The Brains who were near him clustered round, worried and excited. Some of them tried to soothe him and others tried to persuade the men to let him go. There were dozens of voices talking at once and above them all rose the yells of the boy, who was almost hysterical by now.

'I WANT TO GO HOME!'

For about a minute, there was total chaos in that corner of the canteen.

But only for a minute. Then, quite calmly, more of the men walked over. Four of them picked the boy up, ignoring his struggles and screams, and carried him towards the lift. A fifth man marched ahead, going into the lift first.

All at once, the whole canteen was quiet. The Brains stopped talking. They stopped moving. They almost stopped breathing as they waited tensely to see what would happen. Bess slid a shaking hand into Dinah's and held on tightly.

The screen inside the lift flashed suddenly bright with flickering, shifting green lines as the octopus patterns were switched on. The kicking, screaming boy was carried in and his feet were lowered so that he was held in a standing position, facing the screen.

Within five seconds, he had stopped struggling. His eyes swivelled towards the screen and stayed fixed there and he stood perfectly straight and still, with a man on either side of him.

'*Oh!*' said Bess softly.

Robert nodded, and his face was dark and frowning. 'Total control,' he muttered out of the side of his mouth.

OXFORD
UNIVERSITY PRESS

Great Clarendon Street, Oxford OX2 6DP
Oxford University Press is a department of the University of Oxford.
It furthers the University's objective of excellence in research, scholarship,
and education by publishing worldwide. Oxford is a registered trade mark
of Oxford University Press in the UK and in certain other countries

First published 1985
First published in this edition 2017

British Library Cataloguing in Publication Data

Data available

ISBN: 978-0-19-275997-9

1 3 5 7 9 10 8 6 4 2

Printed in Great Britain

Paper used in the production of this book is a natural,
recyclable product made from wood grown in sustainable forests.
The manufacturing process conforms to the environmental
regulations of the country of origin.

THE DEMON HEADMASTER

AND THE

PRIME MINISTER'S BRAIN

GILLIAN CROSS

OXFORD
UNIVERSITY PRESS

CONTENTS

1

THE OCTOPUS GAME

'Dinah!'

Dinah didn't hear. She was settled in the crook of the big, old pear tree, thinking about the website she was designing.

'Dinah!'

She was concentrating so hard that she did not hear the voices calling her from the other end of the garden.

But Lloyd was not the sort of person to put up with being ignored. He came stamping through the garden, with all the others following him, and stood beside the tree.

'DINAH!'

She looked down and blinked at him.

'Oh. Sorry. I was thinking.'

'Huh!' snorted Lloyd.

Harvey, Dinah's other adopted brother, raced up and interrupted, just as Lloyd was about to say something really rude.

'Di, aren't you ready? Look, everyone else is here. We want to get going.'

Dinah peered between the branches. Sure enough, there were the other three members of SPLAT. Two tall figures—Ian and Mandy—hauling along a smaller, chubbier one that struggled crossly.

'Ingrid doesn't look very happy,' Dinah said.

'Ingrid *isn't* very happy!' shouted Ingrid, scowling fiercely. 'Ingrid's sick to death of the horrible Computer Club. We went *yesterday*. Why do we have to go again today?'

'We voted to spend this week at the Computer Club.' Lloyd gave her a stern look that was meant to shut her up. 'What's the point of having a secret society if we don't all stick together?'

But it was not so easy to shut Ingrid up. 'What's the point of having a secret society at all, if we don't do anything special? We were going to have a great time this summer. A SPLAT picnic and a SPLAT camp in the woods and a SPLAT visit to the Science Museum and— oh, lots of things. But we've landed up trotting back to school, like everyone else. To the *Computer Club*.' She pulled a fierce, ugly face.

'It's only for another four days, Ing,' Mandy said gently. 'And if you'd only try to enjoy it, you'd see it's fun.'

'It's *boring*,' Ingrid said firmly. 'And anyway, who wants to go back to school in the holidays?'

'We voted,' Lloyd said again. He folded his arms and glared at Ingrid. 'Now stop moaning and behave properly.'

Up in her tree, Dinah started to get irritated. She didn't want to listen to their squabbling. She wanted to get on with her website.

'Look, Ing.' She waved the paper she was writing on. '*I* haven't forgotten about the rest of the holiday. I'm going to put it all on the SPLAT website I'm making. Why don't you go ahead with the others and make sure we've got a computer? Then when I get there I can show you what I'm doing.'

Ingrid scowled. 'It's still just computer stuff, isn't it?' But she did not manage to sound quite as angry as before, and a moment later, she was letting Mandy lead her out of the side gate and away towards the school.

At the foot of the tree, Ian bowed low, in his usual teasing way. 'Well done, O Genius,' he drawled. 'How brilliant you are at handling people.'

'What do you mean *she's* good at handling people?' Lloyd looked furious. '*I* was the one who told Ingrid to behave.'

Ian grinned at him. 'Of course, of course, Great Leader. How stupid of me to forget. I grovel in the dust.'

'Be more sensible if we started going to the Computer Club,' chipped in Harvey. 'If we're not there soon, I'll have to wait *ages* for a game of Diamond Dragon.'

He pushed them both and the three boys began to walk up the garden. Dinah watched them for a moment. Bossy Lloyd and tall, comical Ian. Having one of their friendly quarrels, while Harvey ran along behind trying to stop them. All quite normal and ordinary. She settled herself on her branch again and gave a private grin. Things were so pleasant and peaceful. Oh, it was going to be a good summer, with no excitements and lots of time to work. Now, where had she got to?

An hour later, she walked up the road towards the school gates, with the design for the website tucked in her pocket. Her pale, thin face was as stiff as usual and she looked almost bored, because her feelings never showed on the outside, but inside her head she was singing.

Lovely, fantastic Computer Club! It meant that she could spend all day working out programs and trying new things, without the others nagging her for being dull and not joining in. And there were four more days of it left!

She was so busy planning what she would do on the other days, that she did not look where she was going. She ran up the school steps and nearly fell over two small, gloomy figures sitting at the top.

'Careful!' snapped Ingrid.

'Thought we were big enough to *see*,' muttered Harvey.

Dinah looked down at them in amazement. 'Whatever is the matter with you two? What are you doing out here?'

'Sulking!' Ingrid said. 'Because of the horrible Computer Club.'

Oh dear, thought Dinah. She sat down on the steps beside them, wishing she was Mandy, who was good at this sort of thing. 'You did promise to come, you know. And *you* liked it, anyway, Harvey. What's changed since yesterday?'

Harvey looked round woefully at her, and she remembered how cheerful he had been as he followed the others away an hour ago. What could have changed him?

'*That,*' said Harvey.

Twisting round, he stabbed a finger towards the glass door of the school. Stuck up there was a huge poster. Across the top, it said in large letters:

JUNIOR COMPUTER BRAIN
OF THE YEAR

Underneath was a picture of a man in a white lab coat. He was very tall and very thin, with thick, pebbly glasses. Somehow, the blurred photograph made him look not quite human. More like an insect. Or a robot. Dinah actually found herself shivering and she gave a stiff little laugh to hide it.

'*He* can't be the Junior Computer Brain of the Year. He's much too old.'

'He's repulsive!' Ingrid pulled an extra-horrible cross-eyed face and stuck out her tongue at the poster. 'He's the Computer Director. The one who's running the competition to find the Junior Computer Brain. Mr Meredith brought the forms in this morning. And the game.'

'And that was it. Whang! Everything *ruined*,' said Harvey miserably. 'Yesterday was great. Like you said. We played all sorts of games and learnt some things as well. But today—well, no one will think about anything except the competition game.'

'They think they're going to win, do they?' Dinah said.

'*No*.' Ingrid looked impatient. 'It's not that. You don't understand. It's not the competition that's taken them over. It's the actual game.'

'But that's silly,' Dinah said. 'A game's just something for fun.'

'That's what we told them,' Harvey said. He sounded really unhappy. 'We told them it was only a game.'

'And what did they say?'

He looked even unhappier. 'They said, "Ssh!"'

'It's made them really *peculiar*.' Ingrid tapped her head and rolled her eyes. 'Remember what they were like when the Demon Headmaster was here?'

Dinah smiled her small smile and tossed her skinny plaits back over her shoulder. 'Oh, come *on*. They can't be that bad.'

Neither Ingrid nor Harvey answered her. They just stood up and hauled at her hands, one on each side, until she followed them into the school and along the corridor towards the Hall.

Dinah let them lead her, but she was still not taking them seriously. Because she could remember what the school had been like when the Demon Headmaster was there. The blank, bare walls. The quiet, hypnotized children moving round like robots. The cruel, bossy prefects. And the feeling of terror everywhere.

That had all changed since Mr Meredith became headmaster. Now it was an untidy, cheerful, noisy school, just like all the others Dinah had been to. How could it have changed back in a single morning?

And yet—it *was* rather quiet today. As they came to the Hall door, Dinah started to feel uneasy. And what she saw when she stepped inside was quite unexpected.

There were no crowds of children charging round everywhere or gathering in little huddles by the computers. There was no laughter or talking. Instead, all the children—about a hundred of them—were sitting crosslegged on the ground, staring up at the big screen over the stage. No one was fidgeting. No one was whispering. They almost seemed to be holding their breaths.

'You see?' Harvey hissed. 'They've all gone goo-goo eyed over this stupid octopus game. Even the SPLAT people. Look at them!'

Dinah could see that he was right. Lloyd and Mandy were sitting on the floor with the other children and Ian was actually at the computer keyboard. He was the one playing the game.

'They've been like that for ages,' muttered Ingrid, getting crosser and crosser. 'One person playing and the rest just staring. It's *stupid.*' Suddenly she lost her temper altogether. She pulled a face at the rows of motionless backs and yelled, '*You're all SILLY IDIOTS!*'

Ian jumped and looked round. Immediately, there was a loud BLUUURP! from the computer. And a wail from the watching children.

'Ing, you're mean,' Mandy said. 'You distracted him.'

'Oh, sor*ry*,' Ingrid jeered. 'What's the matter?

Was he going to be Junior Computer Brain of the Year?'

'Me?' murmured Ian. 'Of course not. I'm just an ordinary moron having fun. I can tell you, it needs a *genius* to win this game. No one stands a chance except—' Then he caught sight of Dinah. 'Oh, there you are!'

'We've been waiting for you,' Lloyd said. He jumped up and began to organize things as usual, catching at Dinah's arm and trying to pull her forwards. 'You've got to have a go at this game. It's brilliant.'

All the others had turned round now. They were staring at Dinah, nudging each other and whispering. Dinah wriggled uncomfortably. She hated people to fuss over her and she wasn't interested in computer games. She wanted to go and work on her own program.

'Come on!' called Mandy. 'I bet you can do it.'

Dinah looked pink and stubborn. 'I don't think I'll bother, thank you.'

'Oh come *on*, Di.' Everyone was shouting it now. 'You've *got* to have a go. You could win the whole competition.'

Dinah felt like a snail dragged right out of its shell. All the children were staring at her and telling her what to do. And it was no good saying she didn't want to. They would never leave her alone until she had a go at their stupid game. Slowly she walked through the crowd towards the computer.

'Traitor!' hissed Ingrid.

'Oh, *Di*!' Harvey looked at her sadly and turned away.

'Shut up, you two,' said Lloyd. 'Just because *you* don't like the game, it doesn't mean that no one else can play.' He pulled Dinah closer to the front. 'You'd better watch first, so you know how to do it. Mandy can show you. She's the best one so far.'

Mandy shook her red hair out of her eyes and smiled across at Dinah. 'I'm not really good. I mean—I can't *do* it or anything. You'll be loads better than I am.'

'Oh, get on.' Lloyd pushed her down into the chair in front of the computer. 'Come on. Start.'

Obediently, Mandy pressed the first key and the name of the game flashed on to the screen.

Octopus Dare.

'It's a treasure hunt,' muttered Ian helpfully. 'You have to steer your way through invisible shoals and then dive down and try and get past the—'

'Ssh!' hissed everyone else.

They had already turned back to the screen, staring with glazed dull eyes. Ian shrugged.

'Sorry I spoke. I just thought Dinah might like to know—'

'Shut *up!*' snapped Lloyd. 'Mandy's concentrating.'

She was. She was frowning and biting her lip as she moved a tiny ship around the screen. Shoals and sandbanks kept appearing and disappearing and her ship looped and zig-zagged frantically trying to avoid them. As each one appeared, the watching children held their breath. And when Mandy managed to steer the ship through them, a sigh of relief went round the Hall.

Dinah managed not to look impatient. She was used to having to wait while people struggled with things that were simple and obvious to her. But—couldn't Mandy *see*? There was a definite pattern to the shoals. Once you'd worked that out, you could go straight through and not round the long way. The thing was a 3-D puzzle that had to be worked out, not a test of quick reflexes. But Mandy obviously *couldn't* see. She went on frowning and steering at desperate speed.

Dinah passed the time by looking round at the faces of the others. They were all staring at the screen with the same eager attention, even though the game seemed quite ordinary. Was it the shoals that they found fascinating? Dinah did not think so. They seemed to be waiting for something else. Something that came later. But why on earth were they so excited about it?

Suddenly the shoals all vanished and a door opened in the side of the ship. Out slid a little yellow submarine.

Mandy sat back and mopped her forehead. 'Phew! I thought I wasn't going to manage it this time. Just let me get my breath.'

'Hurry up,' said Lloyd. 'We want the octopus!'

'Yes! Yes!' everyone else shouted. 'The *octopus*!'

Dinah looked round at them, puzzled by their eager faces. So that was what they'd all been waiting for. That was what the ship had to get past in the next bit of the game. That was what had made them sit so still and watch the screen so anxiously. But—why?

Mandy leaned forward again and clicked on the

submarine. At once, the screen was filled with a pattern of long, waving tentacles. They moved and twisted, twining in a complicated pattern of curves and loops, constantly altering and yet always keeping a balance, swelling and shrinking and dancing . . .

Dinah could not look away. As the curves shifted and changed, her eyes followed them. Backwards and forwards. Up and down. Crossing and uncrossing. It was a strange sensation. Watching them made her feel dreamy and excited, both at once.

Octopus - s - s - s - s! murmured her mind.

It was a second or two before she realized that the submarine was still there, up in the top right-hand corner of the screen. Mandy was trying to steer it past the octopus to reach the sunken treasure. But there was not much time to watch it. In less than a minute, Mandy faltered and the tentacles reached out and engulfed the submarine.

BLUUURP!

Mandy turned round, laughing. 'You see? I'm hopeless. You have a go, Di.'

'Dinah doesn't want a go at your stupid octopus game,' Ingrid said from the back of the crowd.

'She thinks it's boring,' called Harvey.

Dinah stared at the screen. Trying to remember *exactly* what the octopus had been like. Trying to work out how to get past the tentacles. Because she was *sure* it could be done logically, like avoiding the shoals. Only she could not see how, and the problem nagged and teased at her.

'Dinah!' shouted Ingrid. 'Tell them you don't want to do it.'

But her words seemed to come from the other side of a wall of glass. On this side, there was nothing except the octopus. All Dinah could think of was that she knew she could work out the puzzle. If only she could see the octopus again . . .

Almost in a daze, she sat down in front of the computer.

DINAH PLAYS OCTOPUS DARE

'Lloyd!' whispered Harvey.

'Ssh!' Lloyd hissed, flapping a hand to make him go away. 'You'll disturb Dinah.'

Harvey prodded him. 'Ingrid and I are *bored*. Can't we go off to the swimming pool?'

'What? No!' Lloyd pulled a face and glanced quickly sideways. 'Be quiet. Wait until Dinah stops if you want to talk.'

'But she's been playing that wretched game for FOUR WHOLE DAYS!' Harvey said crossly. 'She never stops. And the rest of you just sit and stare at the screen. What's so great about a rotten octopus?'

Lloyd sighed impatiently and forced himself to turn round. 'Look,' he said, 'it's an important competition. Dinah kept the octopus on the screen for ten minutes last time, and she nearly got past it. She could *win*.'

Ingrid came up behind Harvey and her stubborn face peered over his shoulder. 'That's not why you're watching. You're just hooked on the octopus. You *can't* look away.'

Lloyd exploded. 'You don't know what you're talking about!'

'Ssh!' said all the others.

He lowered his voice. 'Why don't you two push off? Go and play Alien Swarm or something on one of the other computers. I'm sick of your moaning.'

'You haven't had a chance to be sick of it,' Harvey said bitterly. 'You've hardly spoken to us for four days.'

He and Ingrid wandered off and Lloyd turned back to look at the screen, just as Dinah brought her ship safely through the shoals. The children leaned forward eagerly, watching as she clicked on the submarine. The click that would bring the octopus to the screen.

Lloyd found himself leaning forward like the others, with his eyes fixed and his mouth open. Out of the corner of his eye, he saw Harvey nudge Ingrid and point to him. Well, let him. They were both wrong. He could look away from the screen whenever he chose. And he would. In a minute. In a minute . . .

Octopus - s - s - s - s!

Quickly and deftly, Dinah began to move the submarine, her thin plaits hanging down on either side of her face, her eyes narrowed. The little yellow shape whirled backwards and forwards and sideways in a complicated dance, just out of reach of the weaving tentacles.

Lloyd felt his fingernails digging into the palms of his hands. He had forgotten all about looking away. All about Harvey and Ingrid. He could not think of anything except the octopus.

The tentacles were flying faster now and it seemed impossible for the submarine to escape. But each time, just before the octopus snatched it, it darted away in complicated loops. More and more complicated each time.

With a shock, Lloyd realized that he did not want Dinah to win. And he did not want her to lose. He just wanted her to keep on and on playing, whirling her submarine free so that the octopus stayed on the screen, waving and wheeling and winding . . .

But Dinah was too good. In a final, nerve-racking rush, she doubled the speed of her movements and her four days of practice triumphed at last. The submarine soared up in a great arc, over the top of the curling tentacles and down the side to reach the sunken treasure. It was there!

At once, the computer seemed to go mad. It began to play a loud marching tune and the screen filled with hundreds of tiny, bright fish. They swam together to form one huge word.

WINNER!

For a moment there was a total, awed silence. Then Lloyd yelled, 'She's done it! Di's done it! Someone go and fetch Mr Meredith!'

Ian raced off and everyone else crowded round, slapping Dinah on the back, cheering her and telling her how clever she was.

And Dinah burst into tears.

Lloyd was astounded. Dinah was crying? *Dinah*, who kept all her feelings locked away like the Crown Jewels? He couldn't understand it at all. It was Mandy who took control of the situation. Waving everyone back, she put her arm round Dinah's shoulders.

'It's all right, Di, don't worry. It's just a reaction, because you've been concentrating so hard.'

Dinah sniffed. 'No, it's not that.' She shook her head from side to side and wiped her eyes fiercely. 'It's just—well, I know it sounds silly, but this has been the most *fantastic* problem to solve. I haven't thought about anything else since I started. And now it's finished. What am I going to do without the *octopus*?'

'You see?' said Ingrid, loudly and rudely from somewhere near the back. But no one took any notice of her, because, at that moment, Mr Meredith, the headmaster, came bustling across the Hall, chattering to Ian.

He was a short, fat man, so enthusiastic that the sight of him set everyone grinning. The children had found it very hard to get used to him, after the Demon Headmaster. Mr Meredith was popular, but it was hard to believe that he was really in charge of the school.

Now he was chuckling with delight as he pushed his way through the crowd and bent to examine the computer, which was still playing its triumphant march while the little fish swam all over the screen, forming and re-forming the same word.

WINNER!

'Well, well, well,' he said, rubbing his hands together. 'My goodness me. Fancy you being so clever. Well done, Dinah.'

Dinah was her usual controlled self again. 'Thank you, sir,' she said calmly.

'Well, well, well.' Mr Meredith shook his head from

side to side as though he could hardly believe what he saw. 'I suppose you'll be wanting me to find the forms now, eh? To send off to the Computer Director to say that you've qualified for the final of the competition? Mmm?'

Dinah hesitated.

Lloyd knew what she was thinking. She hated people to make a fuss about how clever she was. He couldn't understand it. If he were as clever as that—well, of course he *was* in his own way, but if he were clever in *her* way—he'd be standing on top of the town Clock Tower, shouting about it. It really annoyed him when she kept quiet and pretended to be ordinary.

'Yes, she does want to go into the final,' he said loudly. 'Find her a form, sir.'

Mr Meredith looked at him and then at Dinah, with unexpected shrewdness, but all he said was, 'Well, well, a modest girl. Nice to see.'

Then he began to rummage in his pockets, taking out pens and rubber bands and handkerchiefs, while children scrabbled round on the floor, picking up things he dropped. Finally, with a flourish, he produced a sheaf of papers from an inside pocket. Half of them slipped through his fingers and fluttered to the ground, but he only laughed when people bent down to pick them up.

'Doesn't matter. Unless lots of you were thinking of going on to the final.'

'Us? Win *Octopus Dare*?' Ian pulled a comic, horrified face. 'If it took Dinah four days, none of us will ever do it.'

Mr Meredith grinned and started to fill in one of the forms with Dinah's name, age, and address. He signed it with his big, untidy signature. Then he patted Dinah on the head. 'Better get it posted then. Before I lose it. Eh? Eh?'

He shambled off, followed by most of the children, and Ian gave his slow grin.

'Time to celebrate, I should think. What d'you want, Di? Champagne? Fish and chips and a Coke?'

'Sackcloth and ashes and a plate of cold porridge!' said a hollow voice from the back of the Hall. Ingrid came stalking towards them. Harvey followed her.

'That's a bit mean, Ing,' he said reproachfully. 'After all, it was clever of Dinah to win the game. We ought to congratulate her on that, even if we *are* sick of the octopus.'

'*Congratulate* her? On having her name sent off to that Computer Director?' Ingrid gave a slow, dramatic shudder.

As usual, it was Mandy who moved to soothe everyone. She put one hand on Ingrid's shoulder and the other on Harvey's.

'Cheer up, you two. Just think—it's *over*. We can talk about the rest of the holidays now. We've finished with the Computer Club. And the octopus.'

'That's what *you* think,' Ingrid murmured darkly.

3

THE LETTER

A week later, the doorbell rang while the Hunters were having breakfast. Harvey jumped up to answer it. He loved answering things—telephones, doors, people stopping to ask for directions in the street. Harvey met them all with a cheerful grin on his round face.

This time it was the postman. He handed Harvey a fat bundle of letters and nodded at him. 'Having a piece of toast, were you?'

Harvey grinned wider, brushing the toast crumbs off his T-shirt as he shut the door. Then he wandered back into the kitchen, sorting through the letters.

'You've got one, Mum, and Dad's got five. And—hey, there's one for you, Di!'

'Me?' Dinah sat up, with a small flicker of excitement. She hardly ever got any letters. Only a postcard, every now and then, from the house-mother at the Children's Home where she had lived before the Hunters adopted her. 'A real *letter*?'

Harvey held it out to her. It was in a long, stiff white envelope, with her name and address typed on the front. She took it carefully and began to slide her finger under the flap, running it from side to side.

'Thundering hamburgers!' Lloyd exploded. 'You're

not *natural*! How can you bear to be so slow? I'd have ripped the envelope off.'

'*And* dropped it on the floor,' murmured Mrs Hunter.

'*Mum!* How can you say that? You know I'm the tidiest person in this family. Except for Di, of course, and she's inhuman. Oh, and you and Dad—'

Dinah grinned to herself at Lloyd's typical blustering and lifted the flap of the envelope, sliding out what was inside. It was not a letter. It was a stiff card, like a birthday card. She glanced down at it and her eyes opened wider as she saw the patterns snaking across the front. Twisting, twining tentacles. Curling and rolling across the card so that they almost seemed to be moving. Spiralling and twirling and . . .

Octopus - s - s - s - s!

'Dinah?' said Mr Hunter. It seemed like weeks later. 'Aren't you going to *open* the card? See what it says?'

'I—what? Oh yes.' Blinking and shaking her head from side to side to clear it, Dinah flicked the front of the card back. 'Oh! It's from the Computer Director. The one who organized that competition.'

'Eugh!' Harvey pulled a face and made sick noises into his plate.

Dinah could see Mrs Hunter getting ready to send him out of the room. Quickly, to save him, she started to read her card out loud.

'Dear Miss Hunter,

Congratulations on solving *Octopus Dare*. This makes you one of the contestants to qualify for the final round of the Junior Computer Brain of the Year Competition.

The final round will take place in London from August 28th to September 2nd at the Sentinel Tower, North Island—'

'What a weird address,' muttered Lloyd. 'An island? In the middle of London?'

But Dinah had been skimming on, ahead of what she was reading, and all at once she saw something terrible. Her voice died away, and she lowered the card, her hands shaking.

'What's the matter?' Mrs Hunter said anxiously.

Dinah breathed hard and stared down at the shiny, twining front of the card. 'I can't go to the final. Not unless I've got an S-7 computer. And I've never even *heard* of an S-7.'

She stopped sharply and clenched her fists. Because she was beginning to panic inside her head. She was going to miss the final. And there would be beautiful octopus patterns there to solve. She was *sure* of it. She had to go. She *had* to. If she couldn't go she would scream and scream and scream—

She made herself breathe very slowly, to get back her self-control. She *never* screamed. What was she thinking of? Why had she suddenly started to feel so desperate? It frightened her, but she could not stop herself. The very sight of the octopus patterns on the front of the card made her feel that she had to go to the final. She *had* to go, she *had* to go . . .

'*I've* heard of S-7s,' Lloyd said airily. 'They're brand new. Just come on the market. Ginger Frost says his uncle in Edinburgh has got one. Cost about a thousand pounds.'

'Oh, Dinah!' Mrs Hunter looked upset. 'I *am* sorry.'

Dinah screwed up her fists. She wouldn't cry. She *wouldn't*. And she didn't. But instead she heard her voice say, very high and loud, 'Well, you'll just have to buy me one, that's all.'

'What?' Mr Hunter stared at her. 'I'm sorry, Di, but we haven't got a thousand pounds. Not to spare.'

'Well, sell the car.' Dinah was panting. Gasping for breath. 'Mortgage the house. Get a bank loan. I don't care what you do, but you've got to find the money. *I must go to that final!*'

They were all staring at her. All four of them. And she knew why. She was the person who never asked for things. Never made a fuss. Good, quiet little Dinah, who never wanted anything for herself. Only she *did* want this. It was senseless. It was selfish. But the more she gazed and gazed at the octopus patterns on the card, the more she knew she could not bear to turn down the invitation. Whatever it cost.

'Please, *please!*' she shouted. 'You said you'd buy me a bike. Well, I don't want a bike. That's some of the money, anyway. And you must be able to find the rest somehow.'

'It's not that simple,' Mr Hunter said gently.

Dinah was past listening to him. All she could think of was the octopus, the octopus, the *octopus*. And all she could feel was panic. Terrible panic that she might be going to miss bigger and better and more complicated octopus patterns, lacing and weaving and curving . . .

'An S-7!' she yelled. 'You've got to buy me an S-7! I must have one!'

'Dinah!' Mrs Hunter stood up, looking very solemn. 'Please go up to your room until you've calmed down.'

'*I must have an S-7!*'

'Your room!' Mr Hunter gripped her shoulders and turned her round towards the door. 'You'll hate yourself if you go on shouting at us like that.'

'I'll come and see you in a bit,' Mrs Hunter said.

Still sobbing and gasping for breath, Dinah gave a last scream, flung the card at them and ran out of the room. As she went, she heard Lloyd give a low, astounded whistle.

'Wow!' he said.

'Ssh!' muttered Mr Hunter quickly.

Dinah pounded up the stairs, flew into her bedroom and flung herself face down on the bed.

And was quite calm. Instantly.

It was so peculiar that she sat up and blinked, testing out her feelings just as she might have prodded her arms and legs to see if she had any broken bones. There was no doubt about it. She was perfectly cool and controlled.

At once, an embarrassed, miserable shiver ran up

her back, when she remembered how she had just been behaving downstairs. But she squashed it. No point in wallowing in guilt and self-pity. Of *course* she had behaved terribly. She had behaved quite unlike her usual self. But why? And how had she managed to get back to normal so quickly?

She slid off the bed and went to look in the mirror. Her face was still red and blotchy, but the awful screams and sobs seemed a million miles away. Oh, it was annoying that she was going to miss the final, but she quite understood. Of course they couldn't afford to buy her an S-7. And it didn't *matter*. Not enough to shout and scream at Mum and Dad who'd been so lovely to her. Who'd taken her into their home and adopted her.

'How *could* I have done it?' she whispered to her reflection in the mirror.

Think, the reflection seemed to say back. *Think hard. What started you off?*

Dinah stared into the depths of the glass, puzzling.

'It was when I saw the card. From the Computer Director. I was all right before then, and I'm all right now. But as soon as I started to look at the card I felt—weird.'

But what about *the card?* said her reflection.

Dinah thought back over what had happened.

She had opened the envelope perfectly calmly, listening to Lloyd bickering with Mum. She had slid out the card. And—yes—she had still been all right when she did that. Then she had looked down and seen—and seen—

She was nearly there, on the verge of understanding it all, when there was a knock on the door. 'Can I come in?' said Mrs Hunter's voice.

Dinah jumped up and opened the door. 'I'm sorry,' she said awkwardly. 'I'm sorry I made such a fuss.'

Mrs Hunter put an arm round her shoulders and led her across to the bed. 'Sit down beside me, Dinah. I want to talk to you.'

Meekly Dinah sat down. She supposed she was going to be told off. It wouldn't be nice, but she had deserved it, after all. She folded her hands and waited.

'When people start living together,' Mrs Hunter began slowly, '—the way you've started living with us— they have to try hard to get used to each other. Now, you've put a lot of effort into getting used to *us*, Dinah, but I'm not sure we've understood properly about *you*. You're not an easy person to find out about, you know.'

Dinah stared at her, utterly bewildered. 'But you've been lovely to me.'

Mrs Hunter smiled, a little sadly. 'Well, of course we've tried. You're our daughter now, and we want *all* our children to have what they need to grow up properly. But—' she laughed suddenly '—we're not *used* to having a child as clever as you. Perhaps you need more things than Lloyd and Harvey do. Or different things, anyway. Because of the kind of brain you've got.'

Dinah had a terrible feeling that she knew what was coming. 'Mum—'

But Mrs Hunter went straight on talking. 'After you'd gone, Lloyd explained all about this Junior

Computer Brain Competition. We think it could be a really important chance for you. You *ought* to be in the final. And if you have to have an S-7 to do that—well, we'll just have to buy you an S-7.'

Dinah gasped. 'But you can't afford it! You know you can't.'

'Ah.' Mrs Hunter suddenly looked very pleased with herself. 'You didn't know about this, did you?' She put a hand into one pocket of her big, untidy cardigan and pulled out a long, heavy gold chain set with turquoises. 'This is my nest-egg. It belonged to my grandmother. I've never worn it, but I knew I'd need it one day. And if I sell it, I should get enough to buy your S-7.'

Dinah's eyes prickled with tears. She didn't deserve anyone to be so good to her. And she didn't even *want* it any more. Not in the wild, desperate way she had wanted it downstairs. She couldn't let Mum sell her chain for nothing.

'Look—' she began.

Mrs Hunter put a hand over her mouth. 'Not another word. We're going to buy your S-7. We really want to. You just take care of this, in case you need it.'

Reaching into the other pocket of her cardigan, she pulled out the card that Dinah had flung at them. The card from the Computer Director, with the octopus tentacles curling across it. Dinah looked down and saw the swirling patterns.

Octopus - s - s - s - s!

It was no good! She *had* to have the computer,

because she *had* to go to the final in the Sentinel Tower. She had to, she had to, she had to . . .

'Oh, Mum,' she whispered, as she felt the panic starting again, 'I'm scared.'

'You funny girl.' Mrs Hunter laughed. 'What is there to be scared of?'

She did not get an answer. Instead Dinah, who never showed her feelings, hugged her hard and buried her face in the big, untidy cardigan.

4

NORTH ISLAND

Dinah looked round at the SPLAT meeting and took a deep breath. 'I need help,' she said quietly.

'Help? You?' Lloyd stared at her. He could never remember her asking for anything like that before.

She wriggled awkwardly on her chair. 'I'm sorry, but I do. It's this competition. I feel—'

'Not the *competition*!' Ingrid gave a loud disgusted snort and rolled over on the floor, burying her head under a cushion. 'I don't want to hear *anything* about the creepy Computer Director and his smelly competition.'

'Nor do I.' Harvey put his fingers in his ears. 'They've ruined enough of the holiday already.'

Lloyd sighed. No one would think this was supposed to be a serious meeting! Ingrid and Harvey were behaving like three year olds; Mandy, who hated quarrelling, looked ready to burst into tears; and Dinah had turned very pale and stiff.

'It doesn't matter,' she said in a small voice. 'Forget it. I'm sorry I spoke.'

'Of course it matters!' spluttered Lloyd. 'This is supposed to be a secret society, not a playgroup.' He nodded to Ian. 'Help me sort these two out.'

There was a short scuffle, with grunts from Harvey

and loud, dramatic shrieks from Ingrid. Two minutes later everyone was sitting very still and solemn, staring at Dinah.

'*Right,*' said Lloyd. 'Now, what is it?'

Dinah looked even stiffer and more embarrassed. 'It's this final. I can't explain why—I don't *know* why—but I'm scared of it. There's something wrong, something I can't understand. And the nearer it gets, the more nervous I feel.'

'What a stupid problem!' Ingrid said loudly, before anyone else had a chance to speak. 'It's obvious what you've got to do. Just don't go if you don't want to. No one can force you to.'

Dinah shook her head, looking miserable. 'It's not that simple. Mum and Dad have bought me this S-7 computer just so that I can go to the final. It was really expensive. I can't suddenly turn round and tell them I've changed my mind. And anyway, I haven't changed my mind. I still want to go to the final. Every time I look at that invitation card, I feel as though I'll *die* if I don't go. But—I'm scared. I want you all to come with me.'

For a moment there was complete silence. Then three voices burst out at once.

'No one would let us—' said Lloyd.

'Why should we want to—?' shrieked Harvey.

'*I'm not going near the Computer Director* —' yelled Ingrid.

Dinah looked even more miserable, and Mandy got up and put an arm round her shoulders. 'I think we should try and go,' she said stoutly. 'Dinah wouldn't have asked us unless she felt *really* upset. And I bet you could make a plan if you tried, Lloyd. You could say *we* all want a trip to London too. If Dinah's getting one. We could go and stay with your Auntie Alice and visit the Science Museum.'

Lloyd was tempted. He loved organizing things. Especially huge, complicated plans. A SPLAT trip to London! That would really be something. Only—Ingrid and Harvey were still looking rebellious.

Then, unexpectedly, Ian spoke. Until then, he had been lounging back in his chair, looking slightly superior. But now he jumped to his feet, taking them all by surprise. '*I* think we should try and go, as well. We're being pathetic. Not like SPLAT at all. It's supposed to be a fighting organization. Remember? The Society for the Protection of our Lives Against Them. When we started it, we were strong—the Demon Headmaster couldn't hypnotize any of us except Dinah, and we defeated his plans. But look at us now! We've wasted all this morning, just bickering!'

He glared round in disgust, and the others looked sheepish. Even Ingrid stopped pulling a sulky face and hung her head. Ian snorted.

'We need something to do. We've got *feeble*! If the Demon Headmaster came back now, he'd have us all in his power in a couple of seconds.'

He snatched the heavy, plush cloth off the table and draped it round his shoulders, so that it hung in long folds, like a teacher's gown. Then his fair, lazy face set into stern lines, like the face of the Demon Headmaster.

'Funny that you should all be so sleepy,' he crooned. 'Look into my eyes. Look deep, deep into my eyes.'

Ingrid giggled. 'Don't be thick. You don't look like him at all. Even *you* aren't ugly enough.'

'Quiet!' snapped Ian. 'Do not disturb the others. They want to go to sleep.' His voice slowed, soothingly. 'They're so, so sleepy. They can't lift their arms or their legs.'

They all began to play up to him. Mandy let her head slump forward. Lloyd and Harvey flopped sideways and Ingrid gave a snore. Even Dinah relaxed.

'That's better,' crooned Ian. 'Much more orderly. Now, close your eyes, all of you. Sleep, sleep, sleep . . .'

Obediently, they shut their eyes. Ingrid opened one again and peeped at him, but he glared so fiercely at her that she shut it quickly.

'Now,' he said, in quite a different voice, sharp and precise, 'I will give you your instructions. Tomorrow we will plan to take over the world and run it efficiently, but today we have more important things to do. We have to solve Dinah's problem. Everyone repeat after me—we will do our best to go to London with Dinah.'

'We will do our best to go to London with Dinah,' chorused the others.

'And we will succeed,' Ian said firmly.

'*And we will succeed.*'

It was not as difficult as they had expected. On the morning of 28 August, all six members of SPLAT climbed off a train in the middle of London. Feeling tired and thirsty in the dry, summer heat, they dragged their cases up the platform. Dinah had the most to carry, because she had brought her S-7 as well, but it was Ingrid who complained the loudest.

'I still don't see *why* we've got to do this. I don't want anything to do with the Computer Director. Why can't we *really* go to your Auntie Alice's, Lloyd? And visit the Science Museum?'

'We've *told* you,' Lloyd said impatiently. 'Six million times already. We're SPLAT, and we're going with Dinah.' He gripped the back of Ingrid's neck and pushed her up the platform and through the ticket barrier.

'I still think it's mean to trick Auntie Alice,' muttered Harvey.

'Sshh!' hissed Lloyd. 'I'm going to make the phone call.'

He went a little way down the platform, so the others couldn't hear everything he said, but snatches of talk drifted back to them.

'. . . terribly sorry, Auntie Alice . . . *enormous* bright red spots . . . this morning . . . yes, all of us . . . yes, all over . . .'

When he came back, he didn't look very happy. 'Well, that's done,' he said. 'But it was horrid. She was ever so nice and sympathetic.'

'Ah, but you *had* to do it, didn't you?' Ingrid said nastily. 'So that we can be SPLAT and go with Dinah.'

She was still in a really bad temper. When they

went down the steps into the Underground station, she trailed behind, making loud, rude remarks to Harvey. And when they got to the Underground train, she persuaded him to sit up at the far end of the carriage with her, pretending not to know the others.

'Oh *dear*.' Mandy frowned. 'Do you think I ought to go and talk to them?'

'Whatever for?' Ian looked amazed. 'They're having a *lovely* time. You know how Ingrid likes sulking.'

Mandy did not seem convinced, but she settled back in her seat anyway. 'Oh well, they'll probably be all right when we reach North Island. That's what the place is called, isn't it, Dinah? An island sounds wonderful. This horrible, dusty heat is making us all crotchety. Just think how lovely it'll be to see a beautiful river, full of water.'

Dinah frowned. Until then she had not joined in the conversation at all. She had sat, very still and upright, on the edge of her seat, looking wooden because she was so nervous. But now she said, 'I've been wondering about that. Yes, the place *is* called North Island. I've got to go to the Sentinel Tower on North Island. So there must be a river. But I can't work out which one. We won't be anywhere near the Thames.'

Lloyd waved a hand. 'Don't worry. I bet there are millions of rivers in London.'

'Perhaps this is a nice little one,' said Mandy. 'With reeds at the edges, and waterfalls.'

'Oh sure,' Ian said sarcastically. 'And herons and salmon and otters. All in the middle of London.'

Lloyd licked his lips. 'I'll settle for just the water. It's so *hot* in this carriage.'

They sat back, dreaming of cool, clear running water and trying to ignore the rude snorts that came from Ingrid and Harvey at the other end of the carriage.

All at once, Dinah sat up. 'Get ready,' she said. 'It's the next stop.'

'Oi!' Ian yelled down the carriage. 'You two ugly mugs! Get off at the next stop.'

'Huh!' Ingrid tossed her head and she and Harvey turned their backs, but at the next station they did get off, even though it was by a different door. They charged up the steps and through the ticket barrier, ahead of the others, and Lloyd could hear them muttering as they climbed the second staircase, towards the open air.

'. . . horrible computers . . . putrid Computer Director . . .'

'. . . spoilt the whole summer . . . and . . .'

'*OH!*'

They both said it together, as they reached the top of the steps. Stopping dead, they looked from side to side, staring. Quickly the other four raced up behind. Their heads were full of beautiful, refreshing pictures of grass and water and ducks.

'*OH!*' they all said, as they reached the top.

Because there was no grass. Not a single duck. In fact, there was not a river in sight.

Instead, they were standing in the middle of an enormous motorway intersection. The station looked tiny, completely surrounded by bridges and tunnels and cars. Roads looped up above them, high in the air, supported by concrete arches. Roads plunged down, vanishing into the darkness of underpasses. More roads ran round them at ground level, on every side. And the traffic sent up a steady, unbroken roar.

For a moment, they were utterly bewildered. Then Ingrid said triumphantly, 'You see? It's all a load of rubbish. Well, *we're* not standing about here, are we, Harvey? We'll go and sit on that bench over there, until they all decide to be sensible and go to Auntie Alice's after all.'

The two of them marched off and Mandy looked distressed. 'We've got to do something, or they'll get unbearable. Haven't you got any idea where to go, Dinah? What about the instructions in your invitation?'

'Well—' Dinah hesitated. 'They're a bit peculiar. They just say, *Turn to the north and you will see the Sentinel Tower on North Island*. That doesn't seem much help.'

'Ah.' Ian shook his head wisely. 'This isn't a holiday camp you're going to, remember. It's a special session for Brains. I bet the rest of them could work out how to get there. They're probably all knocking on the door now. Horrible little wizened fellows, with great bulging egg-heads. And tiny little pebbly glasses. And backs all bent from stooping over their books. And—'

In spite of her nervousness, Dinah grinned. 'Yes, but what are *we* going to do?'

'We could try the instructions,' Mandy said mildly. 'It's easy enough to work out where north is, after all.

The sun's more or less in the south at this time of day, and there's no missing that. Not in this heat.'

'Right,' Lloyd said bossily. 'Everyone face north.'

They turned their backs on the sun and stared. But what they saw was just baffling. In front of them were more and more loops of motorway, arching up towards the sky and down under the ground. And apart from those, there was only one other thing to be seen. In the exact centre of the intersection rose a tall, modern tower block, high and narrow.

It stuck up into the sky like a finger of light, reflecting the sunshine back blindingly into their eyes. Its whole surface seemed to be composed of large squares of mirror, with no sign of any windows or balconies. And it was completely isolated in the middle of the roaring traffic. Nothing else was visible. Only roads, roads, roads—and that single, dazzling pillar.

Then, suddenly, Dinah said, 'Oh! I'm stupid!'

'She's realized at last!' Ian applauded. 'Well, when you've finished cheering, perhaps you'll explain things to us sub-zero morons.'

'Look!' Dinah pointed straight at the gleaming tower. 'Don't you see? North Island isn't an island in a river. It's an island in the *traffic*. And that's the Sentinel Tower!'

Lloyd and Ian and Mandy looked amazed, but, from the bench round the corner, Ingrid laughed scornfully.

'Call yourself clever, Dinah Hunter? We worked that out ages ago, didn't we, Harvey?'

'Tsk, tsk,' murmured Ian. 'Didn't your mother ever tell you not to boast?'

'But we *did*,' insisted Harvey. 'Look.'

He pointed away to his right. Walking closer to the bench, the others found that they could see a flight of steps plunging down into a small pedestrian subway. At the top of the steps was a notice.

TO NORTH ISLAND.

Mandy shook her head, gently. 'Why didn't you *say*?'

'Why should we?' Ingrid shrugged. '*We* don't want to go near the Computer Director. He's bound to turn out to be a robot or a vampire or something.'

'Well, tough luck,' said Lloyd. 'Because the rest of us are going there now. And I've got all the money. So if you don't come with us, you'll have to sit here and stare at the traffic. There's nothing else to do round here.'

He led the way down into the subway. And five pairs of feet followed him.

5

INTO THE SENTINEL TOWER

It was very dusty in the subway. Dusty and dirty and dry. And the narrow passage was lit by bright white fluorescent tubes which showed up every cobweb.

It was cold, too, and slightly musty. For the first few seconds the cold was a relief, but by the time they had gone a yard or two it made their skin feel clammy, as though they had walked out of the sun into a deep dungeon. And their footsteps echoed eerily ahead of them, the noise rebounding off the hard surfaces of the walls.

'Do you think it's far?' whispered Mandy. Somehow it seemed right to whisper.

Lloyd forced himself to answer in a normal voice. 'It looked about two hundred metres. Going straight across from the station. But the subway isn't quite straight, of course.'

It curved gently, first to the left and then to the right, so that they could not see anything ahead of them except the passage. Ingrid and Harvey shuddered and walked closer to the others.

The end came quite suddenly. The subway bent round, a little more sharply than before, and they were facing a steep flight of steps leading upwards to the open air. At the top, they could see the blinding brightness of the sun, reflected from the walls of the tower block.

Lloyd took a deep breath and then marched up the stairs, slightly ahead of the others. They needed to be given a lead. He could feel them hesitating. He would go first.

As he emerged from the subway, he found himself staring into his own eyes.

For a moment it startled him so much that he could not understand the reason. Then he realized. The walls of the huge tower were not just *like* mirrors. They *were* mirrors. The whole surface, right to the top, was made of mirror panels, and he was looking into the eyes of his reflection.

'Wow!' muttered Ian, behind him. 'What a sight.'

'I think it's stupid,' snapped Ingrid. She pulled her cross-eyed face at the reflections and stuck out her tongue.

Lloyd took another deep breath, ready to give orders, and immediately found himself spluttering. Here in the very centre of the intersection, the air was foul with exhaust fumes. Before he could recover, Ian had turned to Dinah.

'Right, what do we do now? What do your instructions say?'

Dinah glanced down to check. 'It says *Present yourself at the door and request admittance.*'

'Hey!' Mandy grinned. 'That sounds very grand. Do you think there's a butler or something?'

'More likely to be a bouncer,' drawled Ian gloomily.

'A huge, hairy thug hired to keep out unwanted visitors like us.'

Ingrid tossed her head. '*We're* not unwanted visitors, are we, Harvey? We're unwant*ing* visitors.'

'Shut up, all of you.' Lloyd rubbed his eyes, which were starting to smart. He had never known SPLAT be so difficult to keep in order. 'Now listen. We don't know what's going to happen, so we'll just have to take our chance. We'll all go with Di when she requests admittance and if there's any opportunity for the rest of us to get in, be ready to seize it. If not, we'll have to use our wits.'

'But you *will* get in?' Dinah asked anxiously. 'I don't want to be stuck in there by myself.'

'Of course we will,' promised Mandy. 'Now where do you think we go? It just says *the door* in your instructions, doesn't it? Do you think it could possibly mean that one?'

She pointed. The door facing them was a very strange shape. It was about ten feet high, but only about two feet wide, and it was made of metal. Engraved across the middle were the words *The Sentinel Tower*. And that was all. No opening. No handle. No nothing. Only, beside the door, was a small metal panel set into the mirror wall, and, above that, a knob like a bellpush.

For a moment everyone hesitated. Then Lloyd marched over and pressed the bellpush.

'Let's just see what happens,' he said stoutly. 'They can't eat us, after all.'

But what did happen took him by surprise. From

somewhere above his head came a voice. An odd, mechanical voice.

'If You Desire Admittance, Please Punch Out Your Name.'

At the same moment, the metal panel in the wall slid aside, revealing a row of buttons lettered with the letters of the alphabet. Lloyd stared for a moment and then began to press them.

L-L-O-Y-D-H-U-N-T-E-R.

As he finished, there was a short pause. Then the mechanical voice sounded again.

'I Am Not Programmed To Admit You. Please Go Away.'

Lloyd stepped back. 'You try, Di. But the rest of us will be ready. When the door opens, we may all be able to rush in.'

Dinah gulped and then pressed the bellpush.

'If You Desire Admittance Please Punch Out Your Name.'

Again, the metal panel slid aside. With a quick glance over her shoulder at the others, Dinah began to punch.

D-I-N-A-H-H-U-N-T-E-R

A pause. Then—

'Please Step Into The Half Circle In Front Of The Door.'

For the first time, they noticed that the concrete ground in front of the door was marked by a metal groove. It ran in a perfect half circle, exactly the width of the door and a foot from front to back.

Carefully, Dinah stepped over the groove, standing with her feet neatly together and her arms in front of her, clutching the handles of her suitcase and the S-7 computer. The others crowded close, but there was not room for anyone except Dinah in the circle. Still, they were all prepared, holding their breath, ready to charge forward as soon as the door started to swing open.

But it did not swing open. Instead, with bewildering speed, it turned, like a revolving stage, taking the half circle of ground with it.

Without moving a step on her own, Dinah was spun away from them, into the building. There was a brief glimpse of a narrow corridor and then the turn was complete. Dinah had vanished and they were staring at the opposite side of the metal door, which looked exactly the same as the first side. Ten feet tall and two feet wide, with *The Sentinel Tower* engraved across the middle. And there was nothing else to be seen except their own startled faces, reflected in the mirror walls.

'Well,' said Ian, after a moment of stunned silence, 'what now, O Leader?'

'We—we—' Lloyd racked his brains frantically. If you want to be in charge of people, there are moments when you must produce a plan. It doesn't matter what, but there must *be* a plan. And Lloyd knew that this was one of those moments. 'We'll try to get in just like Dinah did,' he said.

He stepped forward again and pressed the bellpush once more. But this time, when the mechanical voice asked him to punch out his name, he winked at the others over his shoulder and punched out.

D-I-N-A-H-H-U-N-T-E-R.

A pause. Then—

'This Person Has Already Been Admitted. Please Leave Otherwise The Police Will Be Summoned.'

'Oh dear,' Mandy said softly, 'it's going to be ever so hard to get in. What can we do?'

'I think we should just go back to the station and get a train to Lloyd's Auntie Alice's,' said Ingrid.

Harvey nodded. 'We can say we've been miraculously cured.'

'But we couldn't do *that*.' Mandy was shocked. 'We promised we'd get into the building and make sure Dinah was all right. SPLAT-swear. We can't let her down now.'

'Well, I'll really enjoy seeing you get inside,' said Ingrid. 'Go on. Show me how you're going to do it without getting us all arrested.'

And she and Harvey sat down cross-legged on the pavement and folded their arms, looking up at the others with irritating smugness.

Lloyd tried to ignore them. There *had* to be a way of getting into the building. There just *had* to be . . .

6

THE BRAINS

When the ground began to turn under her feet, Dinah was too surprised to do anything. She did not have time to shout to the others or jump backwards to safety. All she could do was concentrate on not toppling over. Clutching the handle of her suitcase with one hand and gripping the S-7's case with the other, she was whirled round, away from the sunshine, away from the open air, away from the other members of SPLAT into—total darkness.

It snapped round her as though the lid of a box had slammed shut. She was standing in a completely strange place and she could not even see her clenched hands in front of her or her feet on the floor below.

Automatically, she put her suitcase down and felt behind her, trying to push at the door she had come through. But the wall on this side was lined with metal and the door fitted so perfectly that she could not even find the cracks at its edges.

Keep calm, she kept muttering to herself. *Don't panic.* She couldn't have been brought all this way just to be shut up in the dark. There must be a reason for it. Something must be going to happen. Mustn't it?

But she knew that she could not stay in control of

of herself for ever. She could not have been there for more than a minute, but already the darkness was straining her eyes and she was beginning to breathe faster. Something must happen soon. It must, it must . . .

And then it did. Suddenly, in front of her, a tiny green light appeared, floating in the blackness. She could not tell whether it was near to her or far away. It was out of the reach of her hand when she stretched towards it, but beyond that she had no way of telling, nothing to measure it against in the blackness. It just hovered, staying in the same place but vibrating constantly as though it changed shape all the time. But it was either too small or too far away for Dinah to make out the shapes properly.

Then she heard the mechanical voice that had spoken to her when she was outside.

'You May Advance Towards The Light.'

She shuddered. The sensible part of her mind knew very well that the voice was made by a machine. In fact she knew she could do the same thing with her S-7 if she loaded the right instructions. But—it was hard not to think of that jerky, inhuman voice as the voice of the Computer Director himself. She imagined his mouth opening and shutting like the mouth of a robot, while his pebbly glasses gleamed above.

'Please Advance Towards The Light,' the voice said.

It was hard not to be terrified at the thought of stepping forward into—nothing. But there were no other choices. Dinah bent down to pick up her suitcase and then began to shuffle forward, very slowly, step by step, feeling the ground in front of her with her feet before each move.

Both her hands were full, so that she could not reach out to feel whether there were walls on either side. The floor was covered with something soft, like carpet, so that her footsteps made no noise. Cautiously, she coughed once or twice to see if she could tell by the sound what sort of place she was in. She had an impression of walls close to her on both sides, as though she were in a long, straight corridor, but she could not be certain. The only thing she could be certain of was the green light hanging in the air in front of her. With her eyes fixed on it, she shuffled closer, bit by bit.

And slowly, very slowly, it grew larger as she got closer, until she could see that it was made up of tiny, shifting, snaking green lines of light. Something about those lines made her move faster, trying to get near enough to see them plainly. Her quick walk changed to a trot and then a stumbling, awkward run as the lines came clearer and clearer and larger and larger and she *recognized* them.

She was looking through the darkness at a computer screen. And there, dancing across it, winding and shifting and writhing, were the familiar patterns of not one octopus, but *two*. Two beautiful, complicated octopuses of green light, hovering in the darkness of the Sentinel Tower. Dinah was panting by the time she got close to the screen.

'Stop Now,' the mechanical voice said suddenly.

Dinah put down the S-7 and the suitcase, reached out with one hand to touch the glass of the screen in front of her and then ran her fingers down it to see if there was a keyboard below.

That was the last thing she remembered properly. After that, the beautiful, shifting lines of light held her fast, so that she was not aware of anything else around her. She could only see their twirling and twisting and turning and . . .

Octopus - s - s - s - s!

It could have been a minute later that she came back to herself or it could have been five hours. She had no way of telling. But suddenly the octopus patterns vanished and she realized that she could see.

She was standing in a lift, in a glare of light, with a blank, dead screen in front of her where the octopuses had been. At her feet were her suitcase and the S-7. Behind her, the lift doors were open and from the room beyond came a faint hum of voices.

I'm here, Dinah thought. Wherever *here* was. The air was cool and damp and when she glanced over her shoulder she had a quick picture of a hard, bright room. The windowless walls were covered in white plastic and lined with shiny metal cabinets all the way round. And the whole large room was full of people. Full of strangers. Dinah picked up her belongings, swallowed hard and turned round to face them.

They were sitting with their backs to her, in rows of separate desks, and for a moment she had an impression of inhuman neatness and order. All the desks were identical—white-topped, with shiny metal legs. They were ranged in perfectly straight lines, with the gaps between them as regular as though they had been measured in millimetres. On each desk stood an S-7 computer and in front of each desk was a gleaming white-and-metal chair. Sitting in the chairs were dozens and dozens of children dressed in identical spotless white lab coats, their backs hunched as they leaned over the desks. The Brains.

For a second Dinah stood nervously in the lift, remembering Ian's jokey description of them. Perhaps, if she moved or spoke, they would turn and look at her with identical faces, white teeth and metal glasses gleaming under high, curved foreheads. She stared at their backs, gathering her courage, and then stepped out of the lift. The soles of her shoes clacked on the hard, bright floor outside and at once every head in the room moved as the Brains turned to look at her.

The bright, mechanical tidiness was completely shattered. Every face was different—and they were all looking hard at her, some smiling and some just inquisitive. There were boys and girls from sixteen or seventeen right down to eight or nine. Some of them had dark hair, some of them had fair hair, some were ginger and some were mousy. There were plaits and curls and spikes and crew-cuts and fringes. And the clothes which showed at the necks of the lab coats were just as varied—a hotch-potch of colours and shapes. They ranged from plain school uniform to the height of fashion. Everyone was different—and Dinah found herself grinning round at them all.

Before she could move any further or say anything, one of the girls stood up and launched towards her with her hands held out.

'Oh how lovely to see you I'm Camilla Jefferies and I wondered who was going to come and sit in this desk next to me because it's the only empty one and I thought perhaps there was no one else—'

She was the most beautiful girl Dinah had ever seen. One of the oldest there, tall and willowy with smooth pink and white skin. A great cascade of curling chestnut hair fell down over her shoulders, almost to her waist, and a flood of words tumbled from her lips as though she never needed to breathe.

'—look here's your desk next to mine and this is my brother Robert behind you and Bess on the other side of you—'

Meekly Dinah let herself be ushered across to the empty desk and helped into the white lab coat that was hanging over the back of the chair. Then she sat down and nodded at Robert and Bess.

Bess seemed to be the youngest person there. She was shy and nervous, and she was clutching a teddy bear on her lap. 'Hello,' she whispered, smiling up at Dinah.

'Hello,' Robert said quietly from behind. He looked very much like Camilla only younger. About the same age as Dinah. But he was as silent as his sister was talkative and he did not say anything else, just looked shrewdly at Dinah before he bent over his desk again.

'—have you brought your S-7 oh good well you plug it in here let me show you—'

With a stream of instructions, Camilla got Dinah settled into her desk and then leaned back with a happy sigh.

'Oh isn't this *nice* we're really here and settled and everyone's friendly and it's going to be really fun isn't it—'

'Hrmph!' came from Robert.

Bess gave a pale, polite smile and clutched harder at her teddy bear. 'It seems all right so far,' she murmured.

Dinah knew what they meant. Nothing bad had happened yet, but still, at the back of her mind, was the niggle that had been troubling her for weeks. The feeling that there was something *wrong* about the final—about the whole competition. But she could not think of any way to start explaining it. So she just smiled back at Bess and waited to see what would happen now.

She did not have to wait long. Almost as soon as she was settled the mechanical voice rang out over the room.

'The Computer Director Is Approaching. Please Stand And Be Silent.'

Even Camilla stopped talking, and everyone stood very quietly, facing the front. There was a faint hissing sound from behind them. Dinah decided that was the lift coming back. Then, sharply, making them all jump, the sound of feet in hard shoes stepping out of the lift and walking across the floor.

A double line of men in white coats marched briskly up the room keeping perfectly in step with each other, not looking to the right or to the left. When they reached the front of the room, they spread out in an exact straight line, facing the desks, four of them on one side and four on the other.

In the centre, dominating the whole room, they left a space.

I won't look behind, Dinah thought sternly. *I won't.* Glancing from one side to the other, out of the corners of her eyes, she saw that Camilla and Bess were staring ahead in the same stubborn way. They were too well-behaved to gawp over their shoulders, but they were full of curiosity. They were waiting, the men at the front were waiting, the whole room was waiting for the Computer Director to appear.

Then, from the entrance of the lift, a voice spoke. Very sharp and precise.

'Good morning.'

Dinah stiffened. That voice! She could not believe that she had heard right, but now she did not *dare* look round.

'Now that you have all arrived,' the voice said crisply, 'we shall start work without wasting any further time.'

Footsteps sounded as the owner of the voice began to walk up between the desks. Dinah hung her head so that her plaits fell on either side of her face, hiding it from anyone walking by.

No, she was thinking frantically, *no, no, no, it can't be true*. She was nervous and anxious and excited and because of that she must have made a mistake about the Computer Director's voice. She *must* have made a mistake.

But, all the same, she could have sworn that the voice she had just heard was the same as a voice she knew only too well. One that she had good reason to fear.

The voice of the Demon Headmaster.

7

ANOTHER WAY IN

'Are we going to stand here for *ever*?' moaned Ingrid. 'All you've done, ever since Dinah went in, is talk, talk, talk. And now you've even stopped talking. I'm bored.'

'Be quiet,' muttered Lloyd. 'I'm trying to think.'

'No you're not,' Harvey said. 'You're just hoping an answer will float into your head. We can't wait for that. We've got to *do* something.'

'Well, you tell me what, then!' snapped Lloyd, losing his temper. 'If you're so clever.' Why did people never understand how hard it was to have ideas?

'Boys, *boys*,' murmured Ian soothingly, 'I know you're enjoying your little quarrel, but why don't you stop it and help the rest of us decide what to do? Are we going to try and get into the Sentinel Tower?'

'We *must*,' said Lloyd. 'We promised we would. And Dinah's not an idiot. If she thinks there's something peculiar about all this, I bet she's right.'

'OK then.' Ian glanced round at the other four.

'So—what are we going to do? We've tried everything we can think of to get through this door and it's hopeless.'

'Why not look for another way in?' That was Ingrid. She was sitting sulkily on the ground, with her back against the metal door. 'I know you're all older than me and cleverer than me, but you're being really *thick*. It's no good trying to fool our way in through this door, but there might be another one. Why don't we go and look?'

That's what I was going to say, thought Lloyd crossly. He took charge at once, before things could get out of hand. 'Well done, Ing. That's what we'll do. I'll go this way round the building, with Ian. Mandy, you take Ingrid and Harvey and go the other way. Got your SPLAT notebook?'

'Of course.' Mandy took it out of her pocket and waved it.

'Good.' Lloyd nodded. 'Well, write down everything you see that could be a way in. Even locked doors and tiny windows. *Everything*. I'll do the same and then, when we meet at the back, we'll make a plan. Come on, Ian.'

It did not take very long. Because there was nothing to write down. Lloyd and Ian walked off to the left and down the side of the building without seeing anything that broke the sweep of the huge mirror panes. Not a single window or door. Not even an air vent.

As they came round the corner to the back of the building, they saw the others appear from the far side. Lloyd waved his empty notebook at Mandy and turned his thumb down to show how useless it was. Mandy did the same. Nothing on her side either.

At that very moment they saw it. All together. Not a door, but a wide opening. It led on to a ramp sloping down under the building. They charged towards it and met in the middle, peering down into darkness.

'Of *course!*' breathed Mandy. 'It's the car park. Do you think there's a door into the building from down there?'

'Could be,' Ian said. 'Shall we risk the terrible darkness and the shadows that lurk in the corners?' He pulled a horror-comic face. 'I've brought the SPLAT torch.'

He produced a little plastic flashlight from his pocket and pressed the switch. Nothing happened.

'Should have brought the SPLAT batteries as well,' murmured Ingrid nastily.

'Oh, give it to *me*. I bet I can work it.' Harvey snatched the torch from Ian and began to fiddle with it. After a few seconds, it gave out a pale, feeble light. 'Told you so.'

'Right then,' Lloyd said briskly. 'Here we go. Try not to make too much noise, everyone. I should think there's a terrible echo in there.'

It was like going down into a giant cave. As they walked down the ramp, light faded round them and the car park stretched away into the darkness, a vast, empty expanse with a few cars dotted round it.

'We'll go all the way round the edge,' Lloyd decided. 'Then if there's a lift door or something we'll be sure to find it.'

They began a long, slow trek round the dark car park. Their feet echoed loudly on the chilly concrete floor and their whispering voices floated eerily through the shadows, as Harvey swept the torch beam up and down the walls. But there was no sign of any door.

Then, when they were about three quarters of the way round, they saw a dark hump in front of them, huddled in the next corner. Harvey shone the light towards it and picked out a rounded glass body set on two spindly legs with skis at the bottom. The rotors at the very top sent strange elongated shadows up the wall and the torchlight glinted back off the glass.

'*A helicopter!*' said Harvey. He was so surprised that he spoke in a loud squeak that made everyone jump. 'Look. What a weird thing to find down here.'

Without waiting for the others, he darted forward at a run. Ingrid followed him and before Lloyd could gather his wits the two of them were pulling themselves up into the helicopter's cockpit. There was no door to keep them out and they squashed together into the single pilot's seat, chattering in excited whispers.

'Lloyd!' Mandy hissed, sounding shocked. 'You can't let them do that. Suppose they *break* something? You've got to get them out.'

'Of course I'm going to get them out,' Lloyd said irritably. Why was everyone so busy telling him how to organize things? Even Mandy was getting bossy now. He marched across to the helicopter, feeling his way along the wall with his fingertips. 'Harvey! Ingrid! Get out of there!'

'But it's really interesting—' began Harvey.

'Come *down*!'

'You could just have a look—' Ingrid sounded quite excited, even good-tempered, but Lloyd did not listen.

'Come down at once! How can I organize things if

you two just go off and do whatever you want to?'

'But it's not like that,' protested Harvey. 'We thought this might be important and—'

'—and we've found something ever so odd—' Ingrid said.

'—and it wouldn't take a second if you just—'

'—scrambled up here and had a *peep* and—'

'*Down!*' Angrily, Lloyd reached up, grabbed Harvey round the leg and tugged. 'We're not here to play games.'

Harvey squealed, caught off balance, and lurched wildly. For a second the light in his hand swept out towards the centre of the car park, into the darkness. Then he dropped the torch. It hit the concrete floor with a crunch and the light went out.

At the same time, Mandy gave a tiny scream and clutched at Lloyd's arm.

'What's the matter?' Ingrid said sourly. 'Afraid of the dark?'

'No,' whispered Mandy. 'But I saw *people*. Tall figures. In the middle there, between the pillars.'

For a moment there was a horrible, cold silence. Harvey and Ingrid slid out of the helicopter and stood with the others, shivering. Then Lloyd squared his shoulders. After all, he *was* the leader. 'Stay here. I'm going to investigate.'

Slowly he padded across the floor in the direction Mandy had pointed out. As his eyes grew used to the dark, he started to make out the shapes that she had seen. Three of them, very tall and straight and still.

Very still. Surely people would not be as still as

that? And people would be thinner. These shapes were very solid.

Then, as he came up to them, he saw what they were—not people, but tall metal cylinders. They were about two metres high, on little wheels, and they stood under a sort of overhang like a hood sticking out from the side of the pillar. Lloyd did not need to wonder what they were for. His nose told him.

'It's all right,' he called out, trying not to laugh. 'They're not people. They're *dustbins*. Big ones, like the ones at school.'

He was just turning to go back to the others when suddenly, from above his head, came a loud WHOOSH! There was a sound of rushing and sliding. Then, from the overhanging hood, a great mass of peelings and empty packets dropped into one of the dustbins.

And an idea dropped into Lloyd's head. A disgusting, repulsive, sick-making, *brilliant* idea.

'Hey, you lot,' he shouted. 'Come over here and have a look.'

'Why should we?' Ingrid called sulkily. 'We're not here to play games, you know. *You* wouldn't come up and look at our helicopter, so why should we—'

But Lloyd was feeling so pleased with himself that he did not bother to get angry with her. 'Oh, shut up, Ingrid, and stop being silly. You've all got to come over here. *I know how we're going to get into the building!*'

Ian guessed first. When he reached the dustbins he saw Lloyd standing close beside them, peering up under the hood, and he pulled a face.

'Yuck! You're joking, of course?'

'Of course *not*,' Lloyd said. 'Here, give me a leg-up. If I climb on top of this bin, I'll be able to see better.'

Clambering on to Ian's shoulders, he gripped the rim of the nearest dustbin and hauled himself up. For a moment he was balancing on his stomach over the edge. He caught a horrible whiff of rotting vegetables, potato peelings, and old tea-leaves and for one ghastly second he thought he was going to overbalance and plunge head first into the middle of it all.

Then he had pulled himself up and was sitting on the edge of the bin with his legs dangling and his head up underneath the hood.

'It's all right,' he called down softly. 'There's a chute about eighteen inches wide. I can't see any light at the top, but it seems to go on a long way. And there must be an opening *somewhere*, so that people can put the rubbish in. It should be quite easy to climb if I put my back against one side and walk my legs up the other.'

Ian coughed politely. 'Were you—er—thinking of making this trip alone? Or is it going to be a jolly outing for all of us?'

'Of course you've all got to come,' Lloyd said. 'We're SPLAT, aren't we? We've got to stick together.'

'You didn't stick with *us* when we were investigating the helicopter,' argued Ingrid. 'You wouldn't even listen when we tried to tell you about—'

'Ingrid,' Lloyd said dangerously, 'if you don't shut up about that helicopter, I'll drag you up here and throw you into the middle of the rubbish!' The smell from the dustbin was beginning to make him feel peculiar and he wanted to start climbing. 'Come on, everyone, follow me.'

He turned his back on them all and stood precariously on the rim of the dustbin. Balancing carefully, he leaned back against the inside of the chute. Then he lifted one leg and planted his foot firmly against the opposite side. Right. Now for the tricky bit.

'Of course,' murmured Ingrid innocently, 'if the walls of the chute are too greasy you'll fall straight into the bin.'

Lloyd ground his teeth. 'Of course,' he hissed, 'from up here I could spit straight on your head. Be *quiet*. I'm concentrating.'

Pressing hard against the sides of the chute, he lifted his second leg and planted that foot beside the first. And there he was, wedged across the opening.

Carefully he walked his feet up the wall until they were almost level with his body. Pressing his hands backwards on either side of his bottom, he levered his body up another six inches. Then his feet started to walk again.

It was not exactly difficult, but it was very tiring and he had to concentrate hard. As he got higher, he could hear the others below him, clambering up on the dustbins and then working out how to follow him up the chute. But he could not let himself listen to them. He had to think about levering his body and walking his legs, levering his body and walking his legs, levering his body . . .

He had fallen into a rhythm when suddenly he levered his body up, leaned his head back and found the wall giving way behind him. He was so startled that he nearly fell down on top of the others, but just in time he realized what had happened. He had reached one of the openings in the side of the chute. It was covered by a flap, hinged at the top, and it could be pushed open from either side.

Finding the edges of the opening with his hands, Lloyd gripped them and hauled himself up until he was sitting in the gap, with his legs dangling down. By leaning slightly backwards, he managed to push the flap open a little way with his body, so that he could peer through the opening, over his shoulder, and see what was on the other side of the flap.

It was the most amazing room he had ever seen.

For a moment he could not do anything except stare. Then he remembered the others, on their way up. 'You can come,' he called softly. 'It's quite safe.' Then he pushed the flap open wider, so that he could study the room properly.

It was obviously a kitchen. The walls and the floor were very clean and white and shining. From one side to the other stretched row after row of worktops, covered with food in various stages of preparation. There were pots of potatoes, casseroles full of stew, huge dishes of rice pudding.

But there were no cooks. Instead, long thick rods ran from side to side of the room, just above head height. Attached to the rods were all kinds of mechanical arms.

Some of them were stirring, some of them were slicing and some of them were scooping rubbish together. But nowhere was there any sign of a person controlling them.

Robot arms, thought Lloyd. *Like those machines they have in car factories.* They must all be run by some sort of computer.

It was so fascinating that he just gazed and gazed while the others clambered up the chute below him. Enormous saucepans and casseroles were being lifted out of microwave ovens and lined up on the worktops. Then mechanical arms were loading them on to little heated trolleys which ran along rails set in the floor. When the trucks were full, the doors in their sides shut automatically and they ran silently along their rails into a lift on the far side of the room.

Lloyd was just about to crawl right out of the chute into the kitchen, so that he could investigate the lift more closely, when his eye caught something large moving quickly towards him from halfway across the room.

A thick, strong metal arm, much longer than the others, was rearing up over the tables. On the end of it was a giant scoop. While Lloyd watched, the scoop skimmed the worktops, collecting all the little heaps of wet, smelly rubbish. Closer and closer it moved—and suddenly Lloyd realized what it was doing.

'Watch out, you lot!' he shouted downwards. 'Rubbish!'

'*You're* rubbish!' shrieked Ingrid.

'Get out of the way!' shouted Harvey.

'Please,' Mandy added.

And, from the very bottom of the rubbish chute, Ian bellowed, 'Hurry *up*! I can't bear sitting on this pongy dustbin much longer.'

There they all were, with their faces turned up and their mouths open as they shouted.

And when Lloyd looked back at the kitchen, there was the huge scoop, full of tins and packets and peelings and scrapings, poised over the rubbish chute. Slowly tilting . . .

8

THE BRAINS ARE PROGRAMMED

Dinah sat very, very still at her desk, hardly daring to breathe. Up at the front of the room, in the middle of the men in white coats, stood the Computer Director. Only now she did not think of him as the Computer Director. Ever since he had reached the front of the room and she had been able to see him, she had known who he really was.

He was dressed in a spotless white lab coat, without a single crease, and his eyes were covered by thick, pebbly glasses. He looked exactly like his photograph on the posters that Mr Meredith had stuck up at school. But his voice and the way he walked and the way he held his head were all unmistakable. And Dinah knew that if he took off the thick glasses she would find herself gazing into a pair of strange sea-green eyes. Huge eyes, that had the power to hypnotize her, so that she felt she was drowning in their depths. So that she forgot what happened and did everything he told her. The eyes of the Demon Headmaster.

That was what she had expected, as soon as she guessed who he was. She thought he would start by hypnotizing all the Brains. But she was wrong. Instead, without any introduction or any polite speech of welcome, he had begun to dictate notes in a fast, clipped voice.

Dinah was so paralysed with fear that she had to make a great effort to pick up her pen and start writing. She was terrified that any noise from her, or any tiny movement, might attract his attention. Then he would recognize her, and—and—she did not know what would happen after that, but she knew it would be horrible. Keeping her head lowered, she scribbled down the notes, trying to concentrate on what the Headmaster was saying.

'You will all have noticed the rows of cabinets round the walls,' said the cold voice. 'These are parts of the S-700, the world's largest and most advanced computer. There are other parts, throughout this building, but this room is the centre. The main control room. It was the S-700's voice that you heard when you first entered the Sentinel Tower. Among other things, it runs the building.'

The Brains gasped, awed by the enormous size and power of the S-700. Several of them turned round to gaze at the rows of cabinets, but Dinah stayed hunched in the same position, desperate not to attract attention. And the Headmaster's voice went on.

'You have, I presume, all brought your S-7s with you, according to instructions. And I imagine that you are not too stupid to work out how to connect them up where you are sitting. As well as being microprocessors on their own, these S-7s are now acting as terminals to the S-700. Each one of you is in contact with the most powerful computer in the world.'

The most powerful computer in the world. It ought to have been incredibly exciting, Dinah thought miserably. She should have been sitting on the edge of her chair, longing for a chance to use her terminal. But the only thought in her head was *SPLAT. I do want SPLAT.* Where could they all have got to?

It was no use thinking like that! She gave herself a mental prod. She had to keep track of what the Headmaster was saying. He had started to give details of how to operate the S-700. If she didn't learn *those*, he would be sure to notice her. Bending over her notebook, she began to scribble at top speed, like all the other Brains.

And scribble and scribble and scribble. The Headmaster kept pouring out information without waiting for them to understand or ask questions. It took all Dinah's energy to keep pace with him. Out of the corner of her eye, she could see that Camilla and Bess were just as breathless, scrambling to make a note of everything. And it seemed that the voice would never stop. On and on it went, with every sentence giving another important fact. On and on and on . . .

Until at last, suddenly, the stream of words stopped dead and the Headmaster nodded.

'Right. That covers everything you need to know. In a moment, you will be sent to have your lunch. While you are eating, you should learn these notes. After the meal, you will be starting work on the final stage of the competition and I shall expect you to *know* everything I have told you. Otherwise, you will be sent home.'

Giving another brisk nod, he walked quickly down the room towards the lift. Dinah shuddered as he passed her, but he did not look at any of the Brains. He just strode into the lift and slid away.

'Christmas *pudding*!' said Camilla breathlessly. 'You don't mean he really expects us to learn everything he's told us do you realize he's been speaking for *two hours* and—'

'Silence!' barked one of the men at the front of the room. 'No talking until you are sent down to the canteen!' His voice was dead and expressionless and at the sound of it Dinah shuddered again.

Then she glanced sideways at Bess, to make sure she was all right. But Bess already had her head bent over her notebook, her lips moving slightly as she began to memorize what she had written.

Nursing her wrist, which ached from holding a pen for so long, Dinah flipped back through her own notes. Pages and *pages*! How could she ever learn them? She was already exhausted. She had worked harder in the last two hours than she had ever worked in her life, and it looked as though that was only a start. Help!

The white-coated men were walking down between the desks now, sending the Brains into the lift, two rows at a time. The Brains went solemnly and silently, their eyes on their notebooks and their faces concentrating hard.

When it was Dinah's turn, she went with Camilla and Bess and Robert. The men packed the lift so tightly that none of them could move and then pressed a couple of switches.

Immediately, the door closed and for a second there was total darkness. Bess caught her breath, but before she could say anything a green light came on. The octopus patterns began to writhe their way across the computer screen on the wall of the lift.

For an instant, Dinah felt the uneasy, worrying niggle that had been at the back of her mind ever since she entered the Sentinel Tower. Octopus patterns *again*?

Then, as the beautiful, familiar curves filled the screen, she slid into a daze, watching them loop and arch and intertwine and . . .

Octopus - s - s - s - s!

The next thing she was aware of was the lift doors opening. The Brains blinked as the octopus patterns disappeared and light filled the lift. Then they started to push their way out, looking like any other crowd of hungry children.

They were in a vast, windowless canteen, with long tables set out in line from end to end. Very neat, regular lines. Perfectly straight and evenly spaced. Strip lights glared down from above, filling the room with a harsh brightness, and everything was so clean and hard and shining that it was almost painful to look at.

As Dinah stepped out of the lift, she heard the mechanical voice of the S-700.

'Collect Your Cutlery From The Clean Cutlery Dispenser And Then Sit At A Table.'

The message was repeated every ten seconds or so as they all lined up in a neat queue in front of a slot in the wall labelled *Clean Cutlery Dispenser*. As soon as someone stood in front of it, a bundle appeared in the slot. A knife, a fork, and a spoon, wrapped in a paper napkin. The waiting person took the bundle, but the next bundle did not appear until the next person stepped forward.

Very hygienic, thought Dinah. *No chance for the things to get dirty*. But the efficiency of it made her even more miserable. It was just the sort of thing the Headmaster *would* think of.

She took her cutlery and sat down at a table with Robert, Camilla, and Bess. As she settled herself, she looked sideways at Bess. The little girl was pale and quiet and she had brought her teddy bear with her.

'OK?' Dinah said.

'I think so.' Bess gave her a small, shy smile. 'It was marvellous hearing all about the S-700. I just hope I can learn everything in time.'

'*You* hope you can learn it. Goodness, what about me,' said Camilla, 'I'm the world's worst learner it takes me ages doesn't it Robert and—'

'Hrmph!' said Robert.

Dinah looked curiously at him. The two girls were nervous and excited, but they seemed quite pleased with their morning. Robert was different. His face was sharp and solemn and Dinah wondered what he was thinking. But before she could ask him anything the voice of the S-700 sounded again.

'Please Remain Seated. Your Food Will Be Served To You.'

All the Brains were sitting down now, most of them busy trying to learn their notes. At the sound of the voice, they looked up, wondering who was coming to serve them. Would it be the men in white coats or would it be other people? More friendly people?

But no people appeared at all. Instead, the lift doors swished open and a line of little trucks ran out of the lift and along the floor beside the tables.

'Oh look!' Bess beamed all over her face. 'Aren't they *sweet*!'

It was a comic sight. The trucks were running alongside the tables, stopping at each occupied place. When they stopped, doors opened in their sides. Mechanical arms unfolded, lifted out plates and served hot food from inside the trucks. It was like being served by a procession of fat, square gnomes.

But, after a moment or two, some of the other Brains began to wail from the other end of the room.

'But I don't *like* carrots!'

'I can't eat rice pudding. It brings me out in a rash!'

'I'm a vegetarian!'

The trucks, of course, took no notice. They simply went on serving out the same portions to everyone. Carrots, potatoes, and stew for the first course. Rice pudding and prunes for the second course. Each meal looked exactly the same and each meal was exactly the same size.

'I'll never eat all *that*,' muttered Bess, as she was served. 'It's enough to last me for a week.'

'I'll have what you don't want please,' Camilla said hastily. 'I'd be glad to because otherwise I'll starve to death and it's not that I'm greedy only—'

All over the canteen, similar swaps were going on as people tried to make sure they got meals they could eat. Robert looked grimmer and more solemn.

'You see what's happened?' he murmured.

Dinah nodded. 'The computer's been programmed so that the robots feed us all the same meal. All average portions. And we're not all average.'

'That's right.' Robert pulled a face. 'Worse than school dinners. At least the dinner ladies *listen* when you tell them you can't eat something.'

'But it's quite fun watching all the things work, isn't it?' Bess said timidly. 'Now we know how they all fit into the main computer system. Fancy the Director having programmed in everything we're going to do while we're here!'

'No!' Robert said violently. 'I *don't* fancy it!'

Bess looked hurt, as though he had kicked her. 'What do you mean?'

'Don't we get any *choice* about what we do?' Robert murmured. 'Or are we just another set of things for the computer to control? Like the rest of the robots?' He waved an arm at the figures all round the room. The Brains had sorted out the food and now they were silent except for the sound of rustling paper as they turned the pages of their notebooks. 'Look how we're being forced to work with our meal!' Robert sounded disgusted. 'It's *bad* for us. We're not machines. We're people. We need time to rest.'

'But Robert don't forget this is special,' protested Camilla, 'and if we don't work as hard as we can we'll be wasting it so you'll be sorry if you're lazy and you don't do what the Director said—'

'I'm not lazy,' Robert said quietly. 'I'm worried. It's all too—too efficient. Clean and precise and mechanical. And *controlled*. We're so controlled that we don't even know how we got to this canteen.'

'Oh Robert don't be stupid of course we know we came up in the lift and—'

Camilla's voice died away suddenly as she realized what Robert meant, and Bess finished the sentence for her.

'—or *down* in the lift. But we don't know which, do we? Because we were all too busy watching the octopuses wriggling.'

'Exactly.' Robert nodded. 'Don't you think there's something *peculiar* about the way the Director uses the octopuses to distract our attention? It's as though he can switch off our minds with them whenever he wants to. And that's creepy.'

At the back of Dinah's head, an uncomfortable memory stirred. A miserable, strange memory of herself screaming at Mum and Dad to buy her an S-7 so that she could see more octopus patterns. 'It's like an addiction, isn't it?' she said slowly. 'Like when people get stuck on drink or drugs. We're all stuck on the octopuses. That's *terrible*.'

'It might not be the most terrible thing,' said Robert. He was looking even gloomier. 'The important question is—if we *are* addicted to the octopuses, why is the Director using them to control us? Why does he *need* to control us? *What does he want us to do?*'

9

HARVEY WALKS INTO TROUBLE

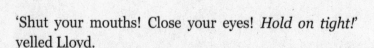

'Shut your mouths! Close your eyes! *Hold on tight!*' yelled Lloyd.

He just had time to screw up his own face before the great scoop full of rubbish tipped right over. A mountain of wet carrot-scrapings showered down on to his hair. Slimy potato peelings slithered over his neck and something that smelt like sour milk dripped down his nose and his chin. On and on went the stream of rubbish. He spat out tea-leaves, brushed flour away from his eyelashes, and peeled burnt rice pudding skin off his cheek. And all the time he was frantically pressing his back and his feet against the sides of the chute so that he did not get knocked down on top of the others.

Their shouts didn't help, either. 'Eugh!'

'Yuck, *yuck*, YUCK!'

'Lloyd, what are you *doing*? Have you forgotten we're down here?'

'*Stop* it, Lloyd!'

As if he was responsible for all the rubbish, instead of catching the worst of it himself. But he couldn't answer or explain, because if he opened his mouth it would fill with muddy water and bits of fat and gristle and eggshells and buttery paper and . . .

As soon as the flood of rubbish stopped, Lloyd gripped the edge of the opening behind him and flung himself backwards through it.

'Come on quickly!' he called down the shaft. 'Before it happens again.'

One by one, the others appeared through the flap. They were soggy and bedraggled and very, very angry. But as they crawled out of the chute and into the kitchen, their faces changed. Their eyes opened wide and they gaped.

'Exploding eggshells!' said Harvey. 'What sort of place is this?'

'It's wonderful,' breathed Mandy. 'I've never seen anything like it.'

Even Ian, who was always so cool, gave a low whistle when he saw the robot arms swinging and bending around as they cleaned up the kitchen. Only Ingrid was not impressed.

'More horrible, loopy arms!' She pulled a sick face. 'Just like the beastly octopuses. I knew how it would be, from the moment we looked inside the helicopter and saw—'

'Ingrid, will you shut *up* about the helicopter!' Lloyd said fiercely. 'We don't want to listen to you moaning on and on. We've got to get out of this place.' He glanced across the room. 'There's a lift over there. I saw a whole lot of trucks of food going into it a little while ago. Perhaps we could—'

'Not *yet!*' wailed Mandy. 'We can't go anywhere looking like this. We're—we're disgusting!'

Lloyd looked. At any other time it would have been funny. Harvey had bits of potato peel in his hair and the front of Ian's white T-shirt was spattered with tea-leaves. Ingrid's face was streaked with flour and gravy. Even Mandy, who was always so neat, had carrot-scrapings nestling among her red curls.

'You do look a bit—strange,' Lloyd said.

'*We* look strange!' Harvey nearly exploded. 'You should just see yourself. You look like a compost heap.'

'Like the inside of a dustbin lorry,' said Ingrid.

Lloyd ignored them and let Mandy brush him down and comb his hair for him until most of the rubbish was out of it. But he was impatient to get on with finding Dinah. As soon as Mandy let him go and started on Harvey, he ran across the room, dodging the robot arms. He wanted to examine the lift.

It did not take long to examine. There was nothing to see, except two smooth, strong doors, tightly shut. Lloyd hunted all round, peering up at the ceiling and crouching down to look along the floor, but he could not find any buttons to press. No handles, no knobs, no levers. The lift might come, but as far as he could see there was no way of calling it.

And it was impossible to open the doors of the lift shaft. Even when Ian and Harvey came to help him, they did not succeed in moving them so much as a crack apart.

'Charming!' said Harvey. He kicked crossly at the doors. 'I suppose we'll have to use the stairs. That'll take for ever. Don't you remember how tall this building is?'

'I don't want to bring tears to your dear little eyes,' murmured Ian, 'but it's *worse* than that.' He had been staring round him in every direction. Now he turned back to face Lloyd and Harvey. 'You haven't realized, have you? There *aren't* any stairs. Look for yourselves. The lift is the only way up.'

Harvey suddenly looked very pale. 'You mean— we're trapped in here?'

For a moment, Lloyd made the same mistake. *I was the one who brought us all here*, he thought. *And now we may never get out.*

Then Ingrid spoke scornfully. 'Don't be a dumbo, Harvey. Of course we can get out. The same way we got in. And the sooner the better, if you ask me.'

Wriggling away from Mandy, who was trying to comb her hair, she darted back towards the rubbish chute.

Of course! Lloyd thought. *What an idiot I am!* He raced back across the room, chasing Ingrid.

'Stop a minute, Ing! You've got it wrong!'

Ingrid looked round. She had already opened the flap of the rubbish chute and hooked one leg over the edge. 'What d'you mean I've got it wrong? I'm the only person with any sense round here. *I* was the one who remembered the chute.'

'Of course you did,' Lloyd said soothingly. 'And you're right. We are going to use it again. But we're not going down—we're going on *up*.'

'*UP?*' Ingrid looked ready to bite him. 'You mean you haven't had enough of this place? You want *more*?'

'We've got to find Dinah,' said Mandy. 'We promised.' She turned to face the rubbish chute. 'It's not very nice in there, but if it's the only way we'll have to use it.'

'It *is* the only way,' Lloyd said firmly. Pushing Ingrid aside, he lifted the flap and clambered through the hole. 'I'll go first. And I'll come out through the next flap. Wherever that is. Right?'

It was harder to start off this time, with nothing solid under his feet, but at last he got himself safely wedged and began to wriggle, walking his legs and levering his body and walking his legs . . .

He had climbed over a metre when it suddenly struck him that he had a long way to drop if he fell now. It was probably six metres or more down into the bin in the car park. One slither, one second's loss of concentration and he would be falling, falling, falling . . .

But it was stupid to think like that. It was no use thinking about what was below. He should be worrying about what was coming. Tilting his head back, he tried to see an opening somewhere in the darkness above him. But there did not seem to be even a crack of light. Nothing but a great pillar of shadowy black, stretching up as far as he could see or imagine.

The opening, when it came, took him completely by surprise, like the first one. Suddenly, as he levered his back up the wall, there was nothing behind him. The flap gave way and he was tumbling backwards and out of the darkness, pushing at the edges of the hole to make sure that he got through and praying that there was no one waiting for him on the other side.

But no angry voices shouted at him. No one squealed with shock at his sudden appearance. Instead, he hit hard floor and uncoiled himself with his back to the room.

When he turned round, for a second he could not make any sense of what he saw. He seemed to be looking down a long, narrow corridor, lined from floor to ceiling with baked bean tins. It was immensely tall—about twice as tall as a normal room—but so narrow that he could have stood in the middle with his arms outstretched and touched the tins on both sides. And why would anyone want to decorate a corridor with *baked bean tins*?

Then, as he picked himself up off the floor and stepped sideways to hold the flap open for the others, the mystery was explained. Because as he moved a few feet to the left he found himself looking down another corridor, identical to the first one except that it was lined with packets of sugar and tea.

Of course! They weren't corridors but the alleys between stacks of shelves. He had come out into a long, high storeroom with rows of tall shelves running from one end to the other. He moved a bit more and saw shelves filled with bags of flour, sacks of rice, tins of tomatoes.

The whole place was cool and airy and spotlessly clean. The floors were polished so perfectly that they reflected the packets and tins above them. And every packet and tin and sack and box was set neatly in its place, next to the others of the same kind, with no waste of space and no squashing together.

'What's up here, then?' Harvey asked, as he came tumbling out of the chute. He picked himself up and peered round. 'What a fantastic place!' Then his expression changed. 'What's that?' he said sharply.

Something large and fast ran across their field of vision, travelling along an alley that ran crosswise, cutting the long, straight rows at right angles. Lloyd stiffened. People? Friends or enemies? He leaned even further sideways, trying to catch another glimpse of whatever it was.

When it reached the alley full of sugar packets, it turned towards Lloyd and Harvey and began to move in their direction. For a second they were both terrified. The thing was a tall, open truck, with sides made of wire netting. It was about six feet high and crammed with tins and packets, and it was hurtling straight towards them.

'Lloyd!' whispered Harvey in horror. 'How does it know we're here? It's automatic. There's no one in there to drive it.'

'Perhaps it picked up the noise you made,' snapped Lloyd. He was just about to call down the chute, to warn the others, when the truck stopped. Robot arms unfolded from the side and began to lift out more packets of sugar. As they picked up each one, they held it for a second and then stacked it neatly in the empty space next to the other sugar packets.

Lloyd let out his breath. 'Phew! It's not after us at all. It's just putting the packets on the shelves.'

Harvey frowned. 'But how does it know *where* to put the packets? There's all sorts of other things in it, besides sugar. How did it know it had to put the sugar packets in *that* place?'

As he spoke, the robot arms picked out a packet of tea. They held it for a moment, turning it round and round, and then the whole truck swivelled and moved a little further along the alley, to reach the space on the tea shelves.

'You see?' Harvey said triumphantly. 'It *knew*. It knew it had a packet of tea this time instead of a packet of sugar. But how could it? It's creepy.'

'No it's not,' Lloyd said firmly. He didn't want to cope with Harvey getting scared. 'It's just a machine. Machines can't be creepy.'

'But how does it *do* it?' persisted Harvey.

For a moment, Lloyd was baffled. Then, as he saw the robot arms turning the next packet of tea over and over, scanning the surface, he suddenly realized. 'It's the barcodes, of course!'

'*What?*' said Harvey.

'Those patterns of thick and thin black lines—'

'I know what barcodes are,' Harvey said impatiently. 'What's that got to do with the truck?'

'It's *computerized*, thicko.' Lloyd felt very pleased with himself for working it out. 'And it's programmed to take the things to the right part of the storeroom.'

Slowly, light dawned on Harvey's face. 'Brilliant!' he said softly. 'Oh, *brilliant*. I must watch it doing it.' He moved away, towards the truck.

'Not yet,' called Lloyd. 'We've got to wait for the others.'

But just at that moment his attention was distracted by Mandy, who appeared through the flap. When he had helped her to scramble clear, she looked round.

'Where's Harvey?'

Lloyd looked over his shoulder, but there was no sign of Harvey or of the truck. Somewhere out of sight beyond the next lines of shelves feet were pattering up and down. 'You all right?' he called.

'Course I'm all right,' Harvey's voice came back. 'It's sensational.'

Lloyd shrugged and raised his eyebrows as he turned towards Mandy again. 'He just couldn't wait until the rest of you got here. We'll have to go after him, but shall we wait until the others have arrived?'

Mandy nodded and put out a hand to help him keep the flap open. While Ian was climbing the last few feet, they could hear Harvey, still moving to and fro.

It was when the three of them were hauling Ingrid through the flap that the shout came.

'Help!' Harvey's voice. Shrill and terrified.

'Where are you?' Lloyd shouted. 'What's the matter?'

'Help! Help! It's got me!'

'Come on!' Lloyd yelled to the others.

They dashed along the baked bean alley, following the sound of Harvey's shouting, turned left and then right and then left again. Then they skidded to a stop, between shelves of dried peas and shelves of spaghetti.

'HELP!' wailed Harvey.

He had been caught by the truck's robot arms. One grab was round his body and one round his left leg. As the others watched, the arms began to lift him high in the air, towards the top of the truck.

'Help! Get me down!'

10

A TASK FOR THE BRAINS

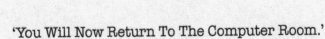

'You Will Now Return To The Computer Room.'

As the voice of the S-700 grated across the canteen, the men in white coats marched out of the lift and down the room.

'Goodness I haven't finished Bess's dinner yet,' moaned Camilla, 'and I'm sure I don't know those notes well enough to—'

'Silence!' One of the men stopped beside their table. 'You will not talk any more until you are told to.'

'But can't I just ask—?' Camilla fluttered her beautiful eyelashes at him.

'No, you may not. Stand up and prepare to enter the lift,' the man said coldly.

'How *horrible*,' Bess whispered to Dinah, as soon as he had gone past. 'He didn't even look at her.'

'Silence!' snapped the man again. He glared over his shoulder, trying to see who had whispered, but Bess was looking very small and angelic, clutching her teddy bear, and he did not suspect her. 'Go to the lift!' he said at last.

All over the canteen, the same thing was happening. Men were giving orders and children were standing up, forming silent queues, and moving towards the lift.

They walked slowly, with their heads bent and their eyes fixed on their notebooks.

'See?' murmured Robert in disgust. 'We're all turning into robots.'

Suddenly, over on the far side of the room, there was a disturbance.

'No, I *won't!*' shouted a boy's voice. 'I'm sick of being pushed around. I don't like the food and I don't like being shut in. I'm going home.'

Immediately, two men in white coats appeared, one on either side of him. Smoothly they took hold of his arms.

'It is not possible to go home,' said the first man.

'You are to stay here until September the second,' said the other.

Both of them spoke in level voices, with no expression. Exactly the same voices they had used all the time. Dinah found herself shuddering. That was how the prefects at her school used to talk. When the Headmaster was in charge. Coldly. Almost like machines. It was never any use appealing to them or trying to get them to have pity or see sense, because they were not free to soften. They were hypnotized by the Demon Headmaster and under his control. And now these men were the same. She was sure of it. However much the Brains argued with them, they would just go on carrying out their orders.

But the boy who was shouting did not know any of that, of course. He shrieked at the men.

'*I want to go home!*'

The Brains who were near him clustered round,

worried and excited. Some of them tried to soothe him and others tried to persuade the men to let him go. There were dozens of voices talking at once and above them all rose the yells of the boy, who was almost hysterical by now.

'I WANT TO GO HOME!'

For about a minute, there was total chaos in that corner of the canteen.

But only for a minute. Then, quite calmly, more of the men walked over. Four of them picked the boy up, ignoring his struggles and screams, and carried him towards the lift. A fifth man marched ahead, going into the lift first.

All at once, the whole canteen was quiet. The Brains stopped talking. They stopped moving. They almost stopped breathing as they waited tensely to see what would happen. Bess slid a shaking hand into Dinah's and held on tightly.

The screen inside the lift flashed suddenly bright with flickering, shifting green lines as the octopus patterns were switched on. The kicking, screaming boy was carried in and his feet were lowered so that he was held in a standing position, facing the screen.

Within five seconds, he had stopped struggling. His eyes swivelled towards the screen and stayed fixed there and he stood perfectly straight and still, with a man on either side of him.

'*Oh!*' said Bess softly.

Robert nodded, and his face was dark and frowning. 'Total control,' he muttered out of the side of his mouth.

'That's what they want. And they're using the octopus pictures—and our addiction to them—to make sure of it.'

The doors slid shut and they heard the hiss as the lift carried the boy off. But even after he had gone, the Brains were quiet, looking pale and solemn, as though they had received a shock.

'What do you think they'll do to him?' whispered Camilla and even she was subdued. 'Do you think they've just taken him back to the Computer Room ahead of us—?'

'No I don't,' Robert whispered back. 'I think something peculiar's going on. And *I'm* going to find out what.'

Dinah felt the back of her neck prickle, sensing danger. '*How* are you going to find out?'

'I'm going to speak to the Computer Director, of course,' said Robert firmly. 'I can't believe he knows how these men are treating us. I'm going to tell him he's got to alter it—or give us a satisfactory explanation.'

'But that won't be any use!' Suddenly Dinah realized how stupid she had been not to tell them all about the Headmaster in the beginning. 'He won't listen to you. I *know* what he's like. He used to be our headmaster, you see, and—'

But before she could begin on her explanation, a man in a white coat was at her side.

'Silence!' he said, in his blank, hypnotized voice. Putting a hand on her elbow, he hustled her off towards the lift.

I must explain to Robert and Camilla and Bess, Dinah thought frantically. *I must tell them about the Headmaster.*

She was so busy clinging on to that thought that she forgot about everything else. As the man pushed her into the lift, squashing the others in behind her, the words thudded in her head. *I must tell them. I must tell them. I must.*

The doors slid shut. As the lift was engulfed in darkness, Dinah looked up at the others, ready to start her explanation again. But she had forgotten the lighted screen. At the very second she looked up, it flashed on, catching her eye, with its fascinating, flickering patterns. *I must tell—*For an instant longer she managed to cling on to what she was thinking. Then everything slipped out of her head as the patterns started to swirl and swoop and sweep and . . .

Octopus - s - s - s - s!

When the lift doors opened again, it was too late. She was swept out as the Brains hurried to their desks. And, even before she sat down, she had seen the tall figure standing at the far end of the room, dominating everything.

The Computer Director was already there, standing very still and straight, with the bright lights flashing off his glasses, so that it was impossible to tell which way he was looking.

Quickly Dinah scuttled into her seat, keeping her head bent and hoping that he would not notice her. If only he did not discover that she was there, she would at least be free to try and work out what was going on and why he had bothered to gather the Brains together like this, from all over the country.

'Good afternoon.' He spoke suddenly, breaking into her thoughts. 'You all had an easy time this morning. Now you must be prepared to work hard.'

'Easy time this morning,' whispered Camilla, 'goodness, he must be joking—'

Mercifully, the Headmaster did not hear her. 'This afternoon,' he continued in his precise voice, 'you will be beginning on the task for which you were summoned here. I will start by explaining—'

'Not for a minute, please!' Robert's interruption astonished everyone. He jumped to his feet and spoke politely but loudly. 'Before we start on anything, I think there are some things we would like to get clear—'

'Sit down,' said the Headmaster coldly.

'But I want to ask a question.'

The Headmaster frowned. 'Questions are an unnecessary waste of time. I shall tell you everything that you *need* to know. I am not here to settle your idle curiosity about other matters. Now sit down. If you speak again, you will be dealt with in a suitable manner.'

Please, Robert, thought Dinah, still keeping her head bent. Terrified that the Headmaster would look down from Robert's face and see her, sitting immediately in front. *There's no point in arguing with him. He's not like that.* But she did not dare to say the words aloud, and Robert had obviously decided that he was not going to give in.

'I'm sorry, sir,' he said, still polite, but stubborn, 'but I don't think this *is* just idle curiosity. I want to know—'

The Headmaster's lips went very thin, pressed tightly together, but he did not speak. Instead, he made a small, sharp movement with his hand.

'Look out, Robert!' shrieked Camilla. 'Oh why did you have to be so stupid you should have guessed what would happen—'

But her warning was no use. From the back of the room, the men in white coats advanced on Robert, picked him up bodily and carried him towards the lift. All the way, he went on shouting loudly, making a speech to the Brains.

'You see? He won't tell us what's going on! And now he thinks he's going to shut me up by showing me those octopus pictures! He thinks we're all so hooked on them that he can use them to control us! Don't let him! Fight back! *Shut your eyes!'*

Even when the octopus pictures began to flicker greenly in the lift, his shouts went on. He stood there with his eyes screwed shut, yelling warnings to everyone. But it made no difference. The lift doors still snapped shut and the lift still carried him off.

Its hiss sounded very loud in the sick, shocked quietness of the Computer Room. No one spoke until, after a second or two, the Headmaster broke the silence.

'Perhaps now you all understand. You are not here to amuse yourselves. You are here to do something difficult and complicated. Something that requires discipline, obedience, and silence. Anyone who disturbs other people will be treated in the way that you have just seen.'

No one spoke. Not even Camilla. They were all too stunned. *It's worse than being hypnotized*, thought Dinah, *because we know what's happening to us. When the octopuses fail, he's using fear to keep us under control.*

'Is there anyone else who wants to make trouble?' said the Headmaster, in a voice of ice. 'Are there any more—*protesters*?' He made the word sound like the name of some loathsome disease. 'If so, let them speak up at once, so that they can be dealt with.'

No one made a sound. Dinah could almost feel the trembling that had come over them all. They might be Brains, but they were only children and they were afraid and confused by what was happening.

'No one?' The Headmaster gave a satisfied nod. 'Then perhaps we can go on without any more stupid interruptions.'

Dinah saw Camilla stir unhappily in her seat and knew that she was worrying about Robert. But there did not seem any point in saying anything. They both picked up their pens, ready to write down what the Headmaster was saying.

'You have all got through the first round of this competition,' he began, 'because you have quick reflexes, you understand computers, and you are good at doing puzzles. Now we are going to go a step further. This puzzle will test your powers of lateral thinking.'

So that's why he hasn't hypnotized everyone! For

the first time in the whole day, something made a tiny fragment of sense to Dinah. *It's no use hypnotizing us and making us act like robots if he wants us to think.* She sat up straighter, alert now. Because the crucial question was—what were they going to have to think *about?*

The Headmaster walked across to the S-700 at the front of the room. His fingers closed round the mouse. For a second or two there was silence as the Brains watched his moving hand. Dinah knew what they were thinking, because she could not help thinking it herself, in spite of everything that had happened.

Would there be more octopuses?

Bigger, better, more complicated octopuses?

The Headmaster straightened at last and the light flashed from his glasses as he moved his head to scan the rows of children.

'The S-700 is now connected to another computer,' he said. 'Through the S-700, your S-7s, too, are connected to that computer. You could have access to it—except,' he paused in the middle of the sentence and waited to make sure that they were all listening eagerly before he finished, '—except that it is protected by a code or a password. I want you to crack the code or discover the password.'

It's impossible, thought Dinah. *We could be here for a hundred years trying to do that.*

'To help you concentrate,' the Headmaster said silkily, 'I should tell you that the boys who have been taken away will not be brought back until you have completed your task. If you want to see them again, you had better begin to work at it.'

Camilla went very white and her eyes widened with disbelief. 'Does he really mean—?' she whispered.

The Headmaster repeated what he had said in even plainer language, so that there should be no mistake.

'I want you to break into the computer.'

11

ON THE SHELF

'Lloyd! Help! Ian, Mandy, Ingrid! Help, help!'

Harvey's voice shrilled out over the huge storeroom, echoing from the rows of tins and the high ceiling. His hands and feet flapped uselessly as the robot arms held him up in the air, two metres above ground. He twisted and wriggled with all his might, but he could not struggle free.

'Help!'

'Be quiet!' Lloyd hissed up at him. 'If you go on yelling, someone will come and find us here. Then we'll be worse off than ever.'

'I *can't* be worse off!' wailed Harvey. 'Ouch! Yerk! Ee-ow!'

Slowly the mechanical arms began to turn him this way and that. One held him steady, firmly gripped, while the other moved methodically over his body.

'What's it doing?' Ingrid said curiously. 'Why is it stroking him?'

'It's not str—spfflt!' Harvey spluttered, as the end of the moving arm tickled his nose. 'It's not stroking me, you stupid lunk-head. It's searching for my barcode.'

Ian looked up. 'I never knew you had one of those.'

'Of course I haven't got one!' snapped Harvey. 'I'm

not a tin of baked beans, am I? Not a—aarrgh! yeeow!—not a packet of rice. Why don't you stop making jokes and *get me out of here*?'

'Oh *dear*,' said Mandy. 'Don't get so upset. We'll think of something. You don't suppose it'll put you down, do you? When it's checked all over and not found a barcode?'

'More likely to sound an alarm,' Lloyd said grimly. 'That's what machines do when they come across something they can't sort out. They call a *person*. We've got to get Harvey down before that happens. Can't *you* do something, H?'

'Oh sure,' Harvey said bitterly. The arms had turned him right upside down now. His legs jerked madly, high up in the air, and his face was slowly turning purple. 'What do you want me to do? Turn myself into a tin of soup?'

'Don't be silly!' Lloyd found it hard to be sympathetic. 'Of course we don't want *that*.'

But Ian's eyes suddenly brightened. 'Yes we *do*,' he said. 'Or something like it. How d'you fancy being a packet of spaghetti, Harvey?'

'Ian!' Mandy shook her head at him. 'Can't you tell that Harvey's really upset? Stop joking.'

'I'm not joking,' drawled Ian. 'I seem to be the only person doing any proper thinking. The rest of you are just running round in circles, twittering like a load of starlings. And the answer's obvious. We should have seen it straight away.'

He turned to the shelf behind him and took a packet

of spaghetti off the nearest one.

'Here!' he called up at Harvey. 'Catch this. If the machine wants a barcode, then *give* it a barcode.'

Taking aim carefully, he threw the long packet of spaghetti high into the air. Reaching out a hand, Harvey grabbed at it, just as the arms began to turn him the right way up again. Quickly, understanding what Ian meant, he found the white square with the pattern of thick and thin black lines which was the spaghetti's barcode. Then he held it out towards the end of the moving arm.

Very delicately, the tip of the arm moved backwards and forwards over the barcode, scanning it. Then, having found what it was looking for, at long last, it stopped its restless searching. The two arms held Harvey still and steady, two metres above ground.

'Phew!' breathed Lloyd. 'That was a narrow squeak. I reckon it was just about to sound the alarm.'

'Thanks, Ian.' Harvey rubbed a hand across his eyes. 'I'm glad *one* of you had some sense. I'll be glad to be down on the ground again.'

'On the ground?' Ian raised an eyebrow, looking amused. 'I'm not sure you've quite understood, Harvey. You see—'

But before he could explain, the robot arms began to move again. Instead of putting Harvey down, they began to lift him *up*. Up and up, higher and higher, until he was fifteen feet up in the air, nearly at the ceiling.

'What?' he shrieked. 'Hey! What's going on?' 'I'm

afraid,' Ian said mildly, 'that you've just told the machine that you're a packet of spaghetti. And it believes you. So it's going to put you with all the other packets of spaghetti.'

'Oh, of *course*,' murmured Mandy.

'Yes,' said Lloyd. 'That figures.'

Even Ingrid nodded wisely, as though she understood. But Harvey was not comforted. 'What do you *mean*?' His voice floated down to them. 'What's going to happen to me? I want to come *down*!'

'All in good time, my little packet of pasta,' crooned Ian soothingly. 'Let's get you safely *up* before we worry about getting you *down* again.'

The arms stretched out, carefully moving towards the topmost shelf. All the shelves below were crammed full, but on the top shelf there was a space about a metre wide, next to all the other packets of spaghetti.

'Don't wriggle, Harvey,' Mandy said anxiously, 'or you'll make all the packets tumble down.'

'Never mind the packets,' moaned Harvey. 'What about *me*? I feel seasick up here. I feel like a tightrope walker. I feel—'

'Keep *still*!' Lloyd called up. Really, Harvey was making a stupid fuss about nothing.

Carefully, the robot arms pushed and tweaked, until Harvey was placed neatly in the gap on the shelf. When he was settled there, they finally unclamped themselves and reached down for the next thing in the truck. It was a large packet of paper. As soon as its barcode was scanned, the truck set off, trundling at top speed towards the far side of the storeroom.

Mandy let out a long sigh of relief. '*Phew!* You were a real genius to think of that, Ian.'

Ian bowed solemnly. 'Don't mention it. Thank you, fans. Just because I look like a brainless hatstand, it doesn't mean I don't have any ideas.'

'Well, how about another one?' came a small, miserable voice from high above his head. Ian turned, with Lloyd and Mandy and Ingrid, and peered up towards the ceiling. Harvey's pale, frightened face looked out from between the packets of spaghetti. 'How am I going to get down from here?'

'Can't you climb down the shelves?' Ian said. 'As if they were rungs of a ladder?'

Harvey looked even more frightened. 'They're terribly far apart. Suppose I fell?'

'You'll have to try,' Lloyd said firmly. He was just about to order Harvey to start when he had a better idea. 'Hang on a minute, though. While you're up there, you might as well be useful. Have a look round. What can you see?'

'Much too much!' wailed Harvey. 'I want to come *down*!'

'Come on. It could be useful. Tell us what you can see.'

Harvey took a deep breath. 'Right.' He sounded annoyed now. 'I can see baked beans and peas and spaghetti and tins of rice pudding and rolls of paper and stacks of string and light bulbs and floor polish and—'

'Don't be thick!' shouted Lloyd, wishing he could reach Harvey and shake him. 'I don't want a shopping list.'

'But that's what it's like,' said Harvey, in an injured, innocent voice. 'All the way across to the other side. It's a huge storeroom. Not just for food, but for all sorts of things. And there are three or four computerized trucks—like the one that caught me—all busy unloading *more* stuff.'

Lloyd wished he were up there himself. It was so frustrating having to explain. 'Can't you see anything *else*?'

Harvey grinned cheekily. 'I can see shelves and the ceiling and the floor and the doors of the lift and—' Then he stopped dead. And suddenly crouched down among the packets of spaghetti. In quite a different voice, he whispered, 'Hide!'

'What?' Lloyd said irritably. 'What are you playing at?'

'I'm not playing.' Harvey's voice was so faint that they could hardly hear it. 'The lift doors are opening. *Hide!*'

Before any of them had a chance to move, they heard a boy's voice, shrill and desperate, coming from the far side of the room.

'Help! Help! Is there anyone there?'

12

ONLY JOKING?

This is ridiculous, thought Dinah. *Don't they understand? Don't any of them understand?*

She looked round at all the Brains, searching for one of them, just *one* of them who looked worried. Who might be wondering *why* the Headmaster had given them this peculiar, impossible task. She was certain that what they were trying to do was wrong. The Headmaster did not do things like this for fun.

But no one else seemed troubled at all. All the Brains were crouched over their keyboards, wrestling with the problem. Some of them were juggling with long strings of numbers, working out ingenious codes. Others were inventing complicated patterns of letters, trying to trick the strange computer into giving away some crumb of information about its password. They were all completely absorbed in what they were doing.

They don't think it's real. Suddenly, Dinah understood. They were all so used to playing games with computers, and solving puzzles set for fun, that they did not for one moment think they were trying to break into a *real* computer. They just thought it was another game, that the Headmaster had set up as the final round of the competition. All they were thinking about was winning.

But no one seemed anywhere near doing that. Even from where she sat, Dinah could see the same word flashing up on screen after screen as the strange computer answered all the attempts to communicate with it.

ERROR

ERROR

ERROR

Camilla looked worse than anyone else, more frustrated and more desperate to solve the puzzle. She was bent forward over her S-7, thinking so hard that a deep frown ran up between her lovely eyebrows. As she worked, she was twisting the ends of her hair and chewing her fingernails.

Poor Camilla, thought Dinah. She's *not thinking about winning the competition. She's thinking about getting Robert set free.* But she was not having any more success than the other Brains. The computer answered all her efforts with the same one-word snub.

ERROR

Dinah sighed. She had been looking at the problem herself. Testing out one useless idea after another. But she could not concentrate on it in the same way as everyone else. Because, all the time, the same uncomfortable thoughts niggled away at the back of her mind.

What computer was she trying to get into?

Why did the Headmaster *want* to get into it?

What was he up to?

As she shifted unhappily in her chair, she glanced up at the Headmaster. He was just turning towards her part of the room. Help! It was dangerous to sit here doing nothing. At any moment his eyes would reach her. If she was not working, he would notice her and—and—Dinah switched her S-7 on again and began to tap the keys. Letters flashed up as the strange computer answered her attempt to get in contact.

WHAT DO YOU WANT?

In the last hour, she had used up a lot of energy staring at that question, thinking up clever, complicated answers. Useless answers. Every one of them had got the same reply. Now she did not even try. She just typed in the first thing that came into her head, so that she would look as if she were working.

PLEASE LET ME IN.

No surprises there. She got exactly the response that she expected.

ERROR

But, out of the corner of her eye, she could see that the Headmaster was still looking in her direction. Head bent, she typed again, industriously.

DON'T BE A MEAN OLD COMPUTER.

That was one good thing about machines. They never got insulted or annoyed. The reply was just as calm as before.

ERROR

Oh well, Dinah thought. *I can keep this up all day.* The Headmaster would never notice, and she would be able to stop worrying about his plans, because *she* was not going to be helping them. She would just amuse herself.

The idea of tricking him, even a little bit, made her feel a lot more cheerful. She went on looking as solemn as before, her pale face just as earnest as everyone else's, but to match her mood she typed in something silly, as a joke.

KNOCK KNOCK

Then she froze. For a second she could not do anything except stare at the S-7's screen. At the words which had lettered themselves across it. It was almost impossible to believe, but there it was. This time, the computer had given a different reply.

The right reply.

WHO'S THERE?

The next line of the joke.

Dinah felt as though an invisible hand had dropped an ice-cream down her neck. There was a slow, cold slither, the length of her spine. Putting out a trembling finger, she typed another word.

DINAH

Instantly, the answer was there.

DINAH WHO?

Was it possible? Was she really going to do it? Half of her mind was screaming, *Stop now, before it's too late!* But the other half would not let her stop. She had to know if she had really solved it.

DYNAMITE-BOOM!

she typed in.

HA HA THAT WAS FUNNY. TELL US ANOTHER.

The words flashed across the screen as soon as she had finished.

What had happened? For a moment she hesitated, not quite sure whether she had managed to break into the computer or not. Then she decided that all she could do was carry on, as she had been told to. Obediently, she started another joke.

KNOCK KNOCK

WHO'S THERE?

OWEN

OWEN WHO?

OWEN ARE YOU GOING TO LET ME IN?

HA HA THAT WAS FUNNY. TELL US ANOTHER.

Oh well. Dinah shrugged and began again.

KNOCK KNOCK . . .

After the third joke, she realized what had happened. She had got herself on to a loop. The computer would go on and on, tirelessly giving the same answers however many jokes she told. Unless she managed to hit on the right joke. The one that would get her off the loop.

In spite of where she was, and the fact that she was mixed up in one of the Headmaster's plans, Dinah began to feel excited. She was sure that she was well on the way to solving the problem. The password was a 'knock knock' joke. The only question was—which one? There must be hundreds and hundreds, and she could not think of any way of choosing. She tried

HARRY UP AND LET ME IN

and

POLICE MAY I COME IN

and

MARY CHRISTMAS I'M A CAROL SINGER

and dozens more, but it was no use. The computer replied to each one, very politely, in the same way.

HA HA THAT WAS FUNNY. TELL US ANOTHER.

This is silly, thought Dinah. *I could spend weeks doing it like this.* What she ought to be doing was thinking, trying to work out how she had hit on the right idea in the first place, and seeing if that would help her. Twiddling the end of one skinny plait absent-mindedly, she sat and brooded, forgetting all about the people round her and the nagging voice at the back of her head that had kept telling her not to go on. All her attention was fixed on one question.

What joke would have been chosen by the person who invented the password? The first stage was deceptively simple, after all. If you wanted to get in, you said 'Knock knock'. It even made a crazy sort of sense. So what else made the same sort of sense? What did you say when you felt as though you would go *mad* if you didn't get off the loop?

Then it came to her. Like magic.

She was absolutely sure that she was right. It had the right feel, somehow. But she could not resist trying it out, just to make certain.

KNOCK KNOCK

WHO'S THERE?

answered the computer.

OLGA

OLGA WHO?

Right. Dinah breathed hard and then typed the answer in, very slowly and carefully.

OLGA MAD IF I DON'T GET OFF THIS LOOP

The effect was so sudden and so startling that she gasped aloud, unable to stop herself. As soon as she had finished, the screen wiped clean and her joke was replaced by a heading and a catalogue of sections. The sight of them filled her with total, paralysing horror.

PRIME MINISTER

PERSONAL INFORMATION

ACCESS TO PM

SECURITY AND PASSWORDS.

She had broken into the Prime Minister's computer. If she wanted to, she could look at all the security arrangements and learn the passwords which would get her in to see the Prime Minister face to face.

And that meant that the *Headmaster* would be able to get in and see the Prime Minister face to face. If he got his hands on the information. The Headmaster would be able to stare directly at the Prime Minister, with his huge, mesmerizing sea-green eyes. And then . . . He must *not* find out that she had solved the puzzle!

But before Dinah could do anything, Camilla, who had heard her gasp, leaned over towards her.

'Goodness Dinah you did sound funny are you sure you're all right you seem very pale and—'

Then she caught sight of the screen of Dinah's S-7 and, before Dinah could stop her or say anything to warn her, she let out a great shriek of delight.

'Oh you're so clever you've *done* it you've *done* it and now we can get Robert back and—'

At the front of the room, the Headmaster turned when he heard her voice. Slowly, he began to walk between the rows, towards Dinah's desk.

THE PRISONER

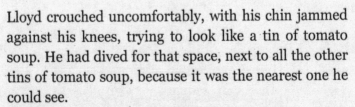

Lloyd crouched uncomfortably, with his chin jammed against his knees, trying to look like a tin of tomato soup. He had dived for that space, next to all the other tins of tomato soup, because it was the nearest one he could see.

When the strange boy had shouted 'Help!' Lloyd had hesitated for a second, like Ian and Mandy and Ingrid, not quite sure what to do. But before they could dash to the rescue, the shout was choked off with an odd kind of gasp, as though a hand had been jammed against the shouter's mouth. From the top shelf, Harvey had pulled a wide-eyed frightened face, frantically flapping a hand to tell them all to get out of sight. So now Lloyd was squashed in with the tins of soup. It was not a very good hiding place, because someone walking past would have seen him instantly, but it was the best there was. At least the alleys between the shelves would *look* clear if anyone glanced down them.

Across the way, facing Lloyd, was Ian, among a lot of packets of dried peas. Mandy was further down, surrounded by staples and paper clips and rubber bands. And Ingrid had vanished round the corner, to squeeze herself between huge boxes of apples.

They were all breathlessly silent, listening to the voices coming from the far side of the storeroom.

'I can hold the boy while you request a rope,' said one man's voice.

It was a curious, dull, lifeless voice. Lloyd frowned, trying to remember where he had heard something like it before, but he could not track the memory down. It was the tone he recognized, not the actual voice.

When the second man spoke, it was in exactly the same tone. 'Is it correct to use the rope? Our information said that the children could be restrained by use of the octopuses.'

'Where the octopuses do not work,' said the first man, 'it is correct to use rope. We are also ordered to leave everything secure when we go off duty this evening. To leave *this* boy secure, we must tie him up.'

'Very well then,' the second man replied. 'I will order a rope.'

In among his tins of tomato soup, Lloyd shuddered. There was something frighteningly cold and unfeeling about the men's voices. And yet—the boy had sounded scared all right. What *was* going on? And how were the men going to *order* a rope?

He should have known the answer to that last question, because he had seen the computerized trolley at work, but he did not remember until a mechanical voice sounded over the storeroom.

'Please Remain Beside The Computer Terminal And What You Have Ordered Will Be Brought To You.'

Of course! That must be the computer's voice, the same voice they had all heard outside the tower. And the trolleys were used to fetch things out of store as well as to stack them away.

Anxiously, Lloyd looked round to see if the rope was anywhere near them. He did not like the idea of seeing another trolley bearing down on him. But he could not see any rope and, after a moment or two, there was a faint hiss of wheels on the far side of the room.

'I have the rope,' said the second man. (What *was* it about their voices?)

'Very good,' the first man answered. 'Help me get the boy back into the lift and then we will take him upstairs to the Restraint Room.'

Whatever the Restraint Room was, it was obvious that the boy did not like the sound of it. Lloyd heard scuffling noises, and the boy must have got free for a second, because there was a clatter of running feet and shouts echoed down the aisles of shelves.

'The Computer Director is dangerous! He is evil! No one is free and—aargh!'

Heavier feet rattled after him and his words were interrupted by an anguished scream. Then the scream, in its turn, was cut short. Cautiously, Lloyd peered out from his shelf, up the alley, driven nearly mad by not being able to see anything.

At the far end of the alley, three figures were struggling. Two men in white coats were trying to get a grip on a boy of about Lloyd's age. A boy with curly chestnut hair, who was fighting wildly to escape.

But before Lloyd could call the others, or decide whether they should attempt a rescue, the men got the upper hand. Wrenching the boy's arms unmercifully behind his back, they dragged him off up the aisle. A moment later, Lloyd distinctly heard the smooth, sliding sound of the lift doors closing and the hiss of the lift moving away. He gave them a second to get clear and then called softly to Harvey.

'OK?'

'I think so.' Harvey looked almost green as he peeped over the edge of the top shelf. 'It was terrible. They *hurt* him. They pulled his arms and jerked his head back and—'

'And did you hear what they *said*?' came Ingrid's triumphant voice. She strolled round the corner, eating an apple and looking pleased with herself. 'Did you hear them talking about the octopuses? It's just like I said. The whole place is riddled with those awful octopuses. All the way up from the helicopter and—'

'Ingrid.' Lloyd only just managed to stop himself from shouting. 'Will you please *shut up about that helicopter*! We've got enough problems, without you driving us all mad.'

'Please yourself,' sniffed Ingrid. She turned her back on the others and crunched loudly at her apple.

Harvey did not even seem to have heard her. He was still talking about the men, babbling on and on in a nervous, shocked voice. 'And the worst part about it was that they weren't angry. They just hurt him mechanically, like robots. That's what this whole building is, you know. A giant robot, all controlled by a computer. And the computer's controlled by the Computer Director. And you heard what that boy said about the Computer Director—'

His voice rose higher and higher as he spoke, and Ian nudged Lloyd. 'What are we going to *do*?' he murmured anxiously. 'We've got to get him down fast. And he's not in any state to climb.'

Lloyd thought for a moment. 'Ropes,' he said briskly. 'If those men could get ropes out of the store, so can we. They'll help Harvey get down safely. *If* we can find them. I don't think we ought to risk trying to use the computer.'

'I don't think we *need* to use the computer,' said Mandy. She took a step backwards, so that she could see the top shelf better, and called gently upwards. 'Harvey! Did you see where the trolley went, to get the rope for the men?'

Harvey nodded nervously. 'It was a great long rope and they're going to tie him up with it and—'

'And we're going to help him,' Mandy said soothingly. 'We'll get him free, don't you worry. But we've got to get you down first. If Ian and I go off to look for ropes, do you think you can watch us and tell us which way to go?'

The unhurried steadiness of her voice seemed to have an effect on Harvey. He knelt up on the top shelf, ready to watch, and when he spoke again, he sounded calmer.

'Go up here to start with. That's right . . . now turn left . . . go along past about three alleys . . . turn right . . .

should be somewhere round about that corner.'

A couple of minutes later, Ian and Mandy were back. They had not simply brought a rope. They had garlanded themselves with ropes, looping the coils on both arms and round their necks.

'This one's to help get Harvey down,' Ian said, 'and the others are for us to take. One each. They should come in useful if we have to go up and down that chute any more.'

'I know it's like stealing,' Mandy said earnestly, 'but we're only borrowing them. And—it's an awful long drop down to that car park.'

'I think we should take everything we can!' Ingrid said fiercely, turning round at last. 'It all belongs to the Computer Director, doesn't it? And he's just as bad as I said he was. I warned you—'

Lloyd gritted his teeth. 'Ingrid, will you *shut up!*' He wished he could gag her. 'Stop wasting time and let's start by getting Harvey down.'

Reaching for the neat coil of nylon rope that Ian was holding out to him, he stepped back, ready to throw it up to the top shelf. 'Watch out, Harvey! It's coming!'

It was the sort of thing that always looked very easy on television. When people threw ropes in plays, they landed exactly in the right place, in reach of the person who was waiting. But it took Lloyd seven attempts. Twice Harvey nearly fell off the shelf and once the rope sailed right over the top and landed in the next alley.

But at last it was done. Harvey held the coil of rope in his hand. For a moment he stared stupidly at it, as though he could not guess what he should be doing with it. Then he got the idea. Wriggling his way along the shelf until he reached one of the upright supports, he began to knot one end of the rope round it.

'Mind you tie it tightly,' called Mandy in an anxious voice.

Harvey nodded, and tested his knot carefully by tugging at the rope before he started to climb down. It did not take long. In a few seconds, he was standing on the ground beside the others.

'Petrified pancakes!' he whistled. 'That was really awful. I feel like a jelly in a jungle.'

'Don't be so *feeble*,' Ingrid said scornfully. 'You ought to be pleased. Now we've got the ropes, we'll soon be out of this place and—'

'What did you say?' Lloyd stared at her.

'Well—we must get out of here, mustn't we?' Ingrid gave a defiant toss of her head. 'You heard what sort of thing was going on. With those men around, we're in *danger*.'

'Oh, *Ing*!' Mandy said. 'What about Dinah?'

Ian walked slowly round Ingrid, looking her up and down. 'You really are a prize specimen, aren't you? You ought to be in a museum. Labelled *Selfish Little Creep*.'

Ingrid tossed her head again. 'I'm not a creep. And I *do* care about Dinah. But what's the use of staying in this horrible, dangerous building, climbing up and down the rubbish chute. We haven't found Dinah yet. We haven't done anything useful at all. I think we should get out and call the police.'

'But what would we tell the police?' Mandy said gently. 'We saw that boy being taken off, but we don't know why. And that's all we've seen. If we start telling the police, they'll probably arrest *us*. For illegal entry and trespassing and stealing ropes and—'

'I think it's *stupid* to go on,' said Ingrid, pulling a stubborn face. 'Ask Harvey. *He* knows. He watched the men knocking that boy around.'

They all turned to look at Harvey. He was still very white and shaken. Mandy put a hand on his arm.

'What do you think? *Could* you bear to go on?'

'It was *foul*,' Harvey said softly. 'It scared me silly watching the way that boy was treated. There's something really *bad* going on in here.'

'You see?' Ingrid put her hands on her hips and looked triumphantly round at them all. 'Harvey agrees with me.'

But Harvey shook his head. 'No, you've got it wrong, Ing. What I said is not a reason for going back. It's a reason for going *on*. We've got to save Dinah, and we've got to *rescue that boy*. Come on, let's get started.'

Picking up one of the coils of rope, he looped it over his shoulder and began to walk towards the rubbish chute.

14

'THE PRIME MINISTER'S BRAIN'

The Headmaster strode down the room towards Dinah. He seemed to tower taller and taller, like a nightmare. She could not move a millimetre. As if she *were* in a dream, she was paralysed by the thought of what would happen next.

But none of her terror could have shown on her face, because Camilla went on congratulating her in the same happy, relieved voice.

'—you're *brilliant*, Dinah, you really deserve to be the Junior Computer Brain and I know it's silly to be worrying about Robert, because he's sure to be all right but I'm so pleased you've done it and he can come back and—'

And the Headmaster can get on with his plans, whatever they are, thought Dinah. Fear was making her stupid. She could see the tall figure getting nearer and nearer and she could see the precious, secret information on the screen of her S-7, but it was not until the Headmaster was almost at her desk that she realized what she ought to be doing. A very simple, obvious thing.

Jerking forward in her seat, she tapped quickly at her S-7's keyboard, ordering it to disconnect and to wipe everything she had just done off its screen and out of its memory. Just in time, as the Headmaster stopped beside her, the screen went blank.

'Dinah?' Camilla said, sounding puzzled.

Dinah sat back calmly, folding her hands together, and waited to see what the Headmaster would do. For a second he did not speak. He stood very very still and stared down at her through his pebbly glasses, without any expression. She kept just as still, not watching him but gazing down at her fingers.

'Well, well,' he murmured at last. 'Clever Little Dinah Glass. How did you get in here? The computer was programmed to keep out anyone called Glass.'

Dinah did not look up. 'I'm called Dinah Hunter now,' she said, in a level, matter-of-fact voice. 'The Hunters adopted me.'

'Extraordinary.' The Headmaster raised his eyebrows. 'People waste so much energy on totally pointless actions. Well, Miss Dinah *Hunter*, what was all the noise about? Am I to understand that you have solved my little problem?' He glanced at her blank screen. 'Apparently not.'

'Oh but she has she has,' Camilla said eagerly, 'I saw the heading on her screen it said Prime Minister Personal Information and that's right isn't it that's what we were supposed to be doing—'

The Headmaster's eyes were suddenly alert. 'So you *have* found the password. I must congratulate you. When I ran a projected feasibility study on the S-700 I worked out that the odds were that *one* of you would discover the password. But not for three days. You have been very quick.' His voice sharpened. 'So—why is your screen blank?'

'Because I'm not going to let *you* get at the Prime Minister's personal information.' Dinah jumped to her feet and looked round the room. All the Brains had stopped working. They were staring in her direction, wondering what the disturbance was about. Raising her voice, Dinah shouted so that they could all hear. 'Listen, everyone, I know what's been going on. We've been trying to break into the Prime Minister's computer. And it's not a game. It's *real*!'

There was an awed gasp and then total silence as they all waited to hear what she would say next. Quickly, she gathered her thoughts. It was no use beginning on a long tale about what the Headmaster had done before. She needed to get the Brains on her side. Quickly.

'I have just discovered the password that the Computer Director wants,' she shouted. 'But that password means *power*. I don't think we should give anyone power like that without knowing why he wants it. I think we should ask the Director to explain what he's up to!'

A rumble of agreement came from all over the room. All the Brains sat back and folded their arms. The message was clear. They were stopping work until they discovered what was going on.

An irritated frown crossed the Headmaster's face, but he did not get angry. Instead, he glanced round the room and then began to make a speech, in a calm, reasonable tone.

'All of you must often have thought how badly this country is run. Money not shared equally among people. Parents bringing up their children on junk food and letting them roam the streets. Inefficiency, strikes, waste. Doesn't it all worry you?'

Heads nodded in every part of the room.

'And haven't you ever thought,' the Headmaster went on, 'that everything could be much better run by one man—one man who cared more about efficiency and order than about his own wealth or comfort?'

Some heads nodded again. Not as many, but still quite a few.

'*I* am that man.' The Headmaster said it quite simply. 'Ask this girl who knows me.' He turned to Dinah. 'Do you deny that I am extraordinarily efficient?'

'No, of course not,' said Dinah, 'but—'

He swept on, not letting her add anything. 'And am I concerned with making money for myself ?'

'No,' Dinah said reluctantly, 'I don't think you are, but—'

Interrupting her again before she had finished, he turned back to face the rest of the room. 'You have heard what sort of man I am. Now I am glad to tell you that I have prepared a vast, efficient scheme for running this country properly. It will be operated from this building by the S-700. Soon, this will be the most disciplined, orderly country in the world.'

'But even supposing all that's true,' Dinah finally

managed to say, '*what's it got to do with the Prime Minister's computer?*'

There was a tiny, tense pause. All the Brains were alert. This was the question they all wanted answered.

'It is difficult to make people be sensible,' the Headmaster said at last. 'They waste time being stubborn and arguing. Claiming they have a right to choose what happens. My plan will cut out all that wasteful choice. Once I have spent an hour or so with the Prime Minister, my scheme will be the *only* choice that people have.'

Bess rubbed her forehead. 'It all sounds rather miserable,' she said timidly. 'I *like* to choose. I like to choose my clothes and my books and presents for my family and—'

'All completely wasteful,' the Headmaster interrupted sharply. 'Once my scheme is in operation, you will wear the clothes you are issued and read the textbooks which will teach you what you need to learn. Presents and other books are simply a distraction from work.'

There was a horrified gasp as people started to understand just what kind of country he was planning. Then Camilla spoke, sounding puzzled.

'But what I don't see is how you're going to persuade the Prime Minister because however good your arguments are and however much time you have to explain, Prime Ministers always have their own ideas don't they and they can't just swap over—'

'He won't be trying to persuade anyone,' Dinah said.

Suddenly she felt very tired and afraid. 'He doesn't need to *persuade*. He can hypnotize people—almost everyone—and make them do exactly what he wants. I don't suppose the Prime Minister's any different.' She could see from the doubtful faces round the room that the Brains did not believe her. Banging the desk with her fist, she spoke more fiercely. 'Don't you understand what we've been doing? We haven't just been finding him a way into the Prime Minister's computer. We haven't just been finding him a way into Number Ten Downing Street, even. *We've been finding him a way into the Prime Minister's brain!*'

'You seem to have grown very excitable,' the Headmaster said. 'But now you have finished ranting, perhaps you will give me the password you have discovered. I'm sure you can remember it, even though you may have wiped it off your computer.'

Dinah gaped. 'You're mad! Do you really think I'm going to tell you? Do you think I'm going to have anything to do with your plans for turning people into robots?'

The Headmaster's lips pinched together impatiently. His face was stern and motionless. But when he spoke again he sounded surprisingly smooth. Almost kind.

'Wouldn't you like to think again?' he said softly. 'It's always a mistake to take important decisions in a hurry, and you have had a very exhausting day.'

Dinah had expected him to start shouting at her. For a moment she did not understand why he was so gentle.

'I've tired you all out, I'm afraid,' crooned the

Headmaster. 'You must be feeling very weary, very sleepy . . .'

Dinah was nearly taken in. She nearly relaxed, thinking that the worst of the danger was past. Then, just in time, she noticed the Headmaster's hand, which was moving slowly up towards his face as he spoke. Ready to take off his glasses. Ready to uncover his eyes.

His eyes! In the split second before they gazed into hers, Dinah understood what the Headmaster was up to. Once he was staring straight at her, with those huge, extraordinary sea-green eyes, he would be able to hypnotize her. He had done it often enough before for her to know that she had no chance of resisting. Once she looked into his eyes, she would be lost, and he would be able to get her to do anything. Even tell him the password.

Just in time, she screwed up her eyes, shutting them so tightly that she could not see anything except the lights that danced in the blackness behind her eyelids.

The Headmaster's voice stopped for a moment. Then he said, 'Open your eyes, Dinah.'

'I *won't*!' Dinah said defiantly, clenching her fists and flinging her head up. 'I know you want to hypnotize me, but I won't open my eyes, and then you can't.'

He drew his breath in sharply, irritated. 'What a tiresome girl you are.'

'You can't make me open my eyes,' Dinah said more quietly. 'Can you?'

There was no answer.

That was more unnerving than any bullying. It was

torture not to be able to see what the Headmaster was doing. But she was not going to let herself get caught by something as simple as that. *It's only a trick*, she told herself severely. *Don't be fooled.*

Even so, it was very dark and lonely standing there with her eyes shut. What could she do next? Could she trust Camilla to tell her when the Headmaster had gone—or was Camilla too concerned about Robert? Would Bess—?

And then Bess screamed. A high, shrill shriek of pain and terror. The sort of noise that cannot be faked. Automatically, Dinah's eyelids flew up. There was no way that she could have stopped them.

'Bess, are you all right—?'

But the second her eyes opened, she found herself staring into the Headmaster's wide green ones. He gave a satisfied smile, dropped Bess's arm, which he had been twisting cruelly behind her back, and began to murmur at Dinah.

'Interesting that you should be so concerned about your friend—when you're so tired. So tired and sleepy that you can hardly hold up your head.

Look into my eyes and feel the sleepiness washing over you . . . '

Dinah felt that she was sinking into the depths of the green eyes. Deeper and deeper and deeper. Until, gradually, her eyes clouded over and her mind blanked out.

15

THE RESTRAINT ROOM

'Dear Mum, I am having a really lovely time in London.'

Ingrid's sarcastic voice floated up through the darkness of the rubbish chute. Wedged uncomfortably between the narrow walls, Lloyd looked down and frowned. 'Ssh!'

But she did not take any notice of him. Just went on muttering in the same cross voice, still making up her imaginary letter.

'You will want to know what we have been doing. Well, we have spent most of our time so far climbing up a dustbin and wriggling up a rubbish chute. Now we are so high that Lloyd has made us rope ourselves together for safety. *Just* like a holiday in the Alps.'

'*Ingrid!*' Lloyd hissed. 'Be quiet! Someone's bound to hear.'

'Huh!' snorted Ingrid. 'Fat chance of that. I don't think there's anyone left in the building except us.'

Somewhere even further below, there was a mutter of agreement from Harvey. They had climbed and squirmed their way so far up the chute that they had lost count of how many floors they had passed, but all they had found was one empty room after another. Strange, cold rooms, lined with metal cabinets.

'This can't *all* be to do with the computer, can it?' Mandy had muttered after the fourth or fifth floor like that.

But there had been no one to answer her. The others just grunted and went on climbing, feeling more and more as though they had got tangled up in the workings of a machine. A spotless, gleaming, huge machine, perfect in every way—and completely inhuman.

They were all getting very tired. Wriggling their way up and down the chute made them use all kinds of strange muscles and they ached in unexpected places.

It's dangerous, Lloyd kept thinking. He had made them rope themselves together, but even so he could not forget the drop beneath them. If they went on like this, sooner or later someone was bound to slip, simply from exhaustion. Already Harvey and Ingrid were getting irritable, and that meant they would be getting careless.

Then, immediately behind him, Mandy sighed. Lloyd was sure that she had not meant him to hear. Mandy never complained about being uncomfortable. But it was a very weary sigh and at the sound of it, Lloyd made up his mind.

'We'll climb out of here at the next floor,' he called softly downwards. 'Whatever there is there, we'll stop for a bit, because we all need a rest. But please *shut up* until then.'

He knew he had made the right decision, because no one attempted to argue. They all whispered 'OK' and went on silently following him up the chute.

It was only another couple of metres to the next

opening. Lloyd squirmed towards it until his head was level with the flap and then pushed it open a crack, so that he could see what was on the other side.

He was so surprised that he nearly lost his grip and slithered all the way down into the dustbin. Because there, on the other side of the flap, almost near enough to touch, was the boy who had shouted and struggled in the storeroom.

He could not shout or struggle now. He was sitting in a chair, tied round and round with rope so that he could not possibly move. A tight, painful gag was strained across his mouth and Lloyd could see a red mark where it had rubbed his cheek sore.

But the really strange thing was his eyes. They were tightly closed, screwed up until they almost disappeared in a tangle of creases. And his head was twisted sideways, awkwardly and uncomfortably. Instead of facing forwards—away to Lloyd's right—he was forcing his neck round so that his face was towards the opening of the rubbish chute. It was as though he was trying not to look at something.

Lloyd hissed, very very softly, to attract his attention. Slowly and cautiously, the boy opened his eyes. And opened them even wider when he saw Lloyd's face, peering round the edge of the flap.

Lloyd pointed at himself and then out at the room, raising his eyebrows to signal *Can I come in?* Instantly, the boy pulled a sharp warning face and shook his head very slightly. The message was clear. It was not safe to come through the flap.

So—what could they all do? While Lloyd was wondering, hesitating where he was, he heard voices coming from the room. Even though the speakers were out of sight, he recognized the dull, lifeless sound of the men in white coats.

'Are both the boys secure?' said one.

'They are,' said another. 'We can leave them like this.'

'Very good,' said the first speaker. 'Then our instructions are to go off duty, as usual. The Director does not require any of us here after half past five.'

'And we report tomorrow, as always, at eight o'clock?'

'That is correct.'

Feet walked across the room, still out of sight, and then Lloyd heard the sound of the lift doors closing and the hiss of the lift going down. This time he did not need to signal to the boy who was tied up. Once the lift was gone, the boy nodded and grunted at him, clearly meaning, *You can come in now.*

Gripping the edge of the opening hard with both hands, Lloyd kicked with his feet against the opposite wall of the chute and pushed himself backwards through the flap. He landed with a bump on the floor, picked himself up and began to hurry over to the strange boy, ready to untie him.

He had only taken a couple of steps when he realized that there was another person in the room. Another boy, of about the same age. But he was not tied up. He was simply sitting in a chair, staring with a blank face straight in front of him. In the very direction that the other boy seemed to be trying to avoid.

Curiously, Lloyd glanced round, to see what there was in that direction. He was vaguely aware that the first boy was shaking his head and grunting frantically, but he did not take any notice. After all, he had already been told that the room was safe. What could be the harm in looking at something?

On the far wall was a big screen, about two metres square. When he saw it, Lloyd gave a smile of pleasure and recognition. Because the green designs that swirled across it were very familiar. Only they were even better than the ones he had seen before. This time there were *two* octopuses curling and weaving and twining. That was worth a second look! In a moment, he would untie the prisoner, but first he must watch the curves and arcs and twists and . . .

Octopus - s - s - s - s!

By the time Ingrid and Harvey reached the opening, it was almost impossible to get out of the chute. Lloyd and Mandy and Ian were all standing just by the flap, perfectly still and silent, staring towards the right-hand wall.

Ingrid came first. She did not waste time arguing. She simply shoved hard at their legs.

'Why don't you shift, you great ugly lumps? Have you gone blind and deaf as well as thick?'

They didn't answer her back, which was peculiar. They simply moved sideways, where she pushed them, and went on staring. Ingrid scrambled out of the chute, glanced round to see what they were gazing at, and gave a loud sniff.

'Harvey, you're never going to believe this,' she called. 'Come and see. It's *pathetic*.'

Harvey had kept close behind her, because he did not fancy being the only one left in the dark. As he climbed out and looked where Ingrid was pointing, he shuddered.

'*More* octopuses! I don't like it, Ing.'

'*I* think it's stupid,' Ingrid said firmly. 'Fancy gawping at them like that, instead of untying that poor boy. Here, Mandy, what do you think you're doing?'

'Mmm?' Mandy turned towards her with a sweet, vague smile and then turned back to stare at the octopuses before she had time to answer.

'You see why I don't like it,' Harvey said miserably. 'Those octopuses really make them go peculiar.'

'Well, *I'm* not putting up with it,' Ingrid said stoutly. Marching over to the screen, she bent and switched off the plug underneath it. The octopus pictures vanished immediately and Lloyd and Ian and Mandy blinked, looking around as though they had just woken from a deep sleep.

'Wha—at? Where am I? How did I get here?' The boy who had been sitting staring at the screen shook his head from side to side and then stood up, gazing at the others with a dazed expression. 'What's going on?'

'There's only one person who looks as if he's got any sense round here,' Ingrid said. 'Why don't we get him untied and ask *him*?'

'Oh, of *course*! Oh, you poor *thing*!' With a horrified gasp, Mandy ran across the room towards the boy who was tied up. 'How *can* we have been so awful? Fancy stopping to watch octopuses while you were still roped up.'

'Not your fault,' croaked the boy hoarsely, as soon as she had loosened the gag. 'It's those octopuses. All I could do not to look at them myself. It seems we're all addicted to them. I think they must echo our brain patterns in some way. And the Computer Director is using them to keep people under control.'

'You *see*?' Ingrid burst out triumphantly. 'It's just what I've been telling you all the time. Ever since we saw—'

'Ingrid,' Lloyd said dangerously, 'if you *mention* that helicopter again, I'll lynch you.' He glared at her until she stopped. It was bad enough having to be rescued by her, without having her going on about how brilliant she was. When she was quite quiet, he turned back to the boy. Mandy had untied him completely now and he was rubbing at his sore wrists. 'Are you one of the Brains?'

'One of the *what*?' The boy grinned. 'Oh, you mean am I in the competition. Yes. My name's Robert Jefferies.'

'I'm Doug Grant,' muttered the other boy, still looking dopey and confused.

Lloyd decided that Robert was the only one likely to answer his questions. 'What's going on in this building?' he said urgently. 'There's something wrong, isn't there? And have you seen our sister, Dinah Hunter?'

'Oh, you're *Dinah*'s brother.' Robert looked surprised. And then very pleased. 'Well, if you're *her* brother, *you* should be able to tell *me* what's going on. You probably know more about it than I do.'

'We don't know anything about anything,' murmured Ian. 'Except the inside of the rubbish chute. We're experts on *that*.'

Robert frowned. 'Well, Dinah seemed to. She said that she knew the Computer Director before she came here.'

'*Knew* him?' Lloyd looked puzzled. 'She never told us that.'

'I'm sure that's what she said. Something about how he used to be your headmaster.'

For a moment there was a frozen, appalled silence. Then Mandy said, in a shaky voice, 'The Headmaster?'

'Well, well, well.' Ian gave a low whistle. 'No wonder he's so good at mesmerizing people with octopuses. That's just his sort of thing.'

Harvey shuddered and sidled up to his brother and even Ingrid looked taken aback. They were all staring at Lloyd, waiting for him to make a plan, to tell them how to deal with this new shock.

But all Lloyd could feel was a terrible rage, so great that his brain would not function. The *Headmaster*! The Headmaster had set up this whole competition and used the octopuses to keep people quiet. And *he* had been caught by them. Him! Lloyd Hunter, who was immune to being hypnotized. Who had set up SPLAT as a resistance group and used it to defeat the Headmaster once before. He had been fooled and drugged with octopus patterns just like any—any stupid *Brain*. It was almost too humiliating to think about.

But there they were, still looking at him and waiting. Even Robert, who hardly knew him, was listening for what he would say. Unless he *did* organize them, they would never get down to anything—and the Headmaster would triumph. Squashing down his black, blinding fury, Lloyd took a deep breath and began to give orders.

'Right then. Now we know who we're facing—and we know how he's been keeping everyone quiet with octopus patterns. Whatever the Headmaster's plotting, it *can't* be good. It's our duty to defeat him and rescue the Brains. So we'll have to be double careful. *And not look at any octopuses!*' He turned to look at Robert and Doug. 'Are you two coming with us?'

'Of course.' Robert nodded vigorously and, after a second's hesitation, Doug copied him, as though he were more afraid of being left on his own than of following.

It took some time to rope everyone up and to explain to Robert and Doug exactly how to climb up the chute, but in the end they set off again on the upward journey that seemed endless. This time, with seven of them, progress was even slower than ever, but Lloyd did not have to remind anyone to be quiet. All the SPLAT members were shaken by what they had just found out and Robert and Doug knew, only too well, what the Computer Director was like. So they were all silent, making no sound except the slow shuffle of feet against the wall and the occasional soft grunt as people heaved their backs upward in the dark.

And that was why Lloyd was able to hear Dinah's voice so clearly. It came floating down from above them, sounding flat and strange.

'Knock knock.'

Harvey gave a small squeak and Lloyd sshhed him as loudly as he dared. The next moment he nearly squeaked himself, when he heard the voice that answered Dinah.

'Who's there?'

The Headmaster's voice. But—was it possible? Dinah seemed to be telling him a joke. A *joke*?

Lloyd felt as though he had gone mad. He tugged gently at the rope, signalling to the others to stop climbing. He wanted to think before he did anything else. To try and make some sense out of what he was hearing.

Dinah's voice came again. 'Olga.' Still in the same expressionless, mechanical tone. Like the voices of the two men in the storeroom and the men in the Restraint Room. Like—Lloyd was still groping in his memory for what those voices meant.

'Olga who?' said the Headmaster.

Then Lloyd got it. Hypnotism! The Headmaster had hypnotized Dinah, to make her do what he wanted. And he had hypnotized the men in white coats. Just as he had hypnotized almost everyone in the school when he was there. That was why Dinah was speaking in such a dull, level voice. She was in a trance.

But why should the Headmaster hypnotize her and then make her tell *jokes*?

Everything seemed even crazier than before.

16

THE COMPUTER DIRECTOR'S TRIUMPH

'You can wake up now.' The Headmaster's voice broke into Dinah's sleep and she woke instantly.

As soon as her eyelids opened, she knew what had happened, even though she could not remember anything. It was obvious from the triumph on the Headmaster's face and from the bewildered stares of the Brains. One moment they had been listening to Dinah defying the Headmaster and shouting about the wickedness of his plans. The next moment, they must have heard her helping him. Telling him the password to the Prime Minister's computer. No wonder they were puzzled.

She had opened the way for him to go ahead with his plans.

Dinah felt as though she wanted to stand up and shout across the room. *It wasn't my fault. I was hypnotized. He's always been able to hypnotize me.* AND THAT'S WHAT HE'S GOING TO DO TO THE PRIME MINISTER! She longed to make the Brains understand that she was not to blame.

But there was no time for that. Not a second to spare on her own selfish feelings. She had to work out if there was anything she could *do*.

Looking up at the Headmaster, she spoke in a small, tight voice. 'What have you done?'

'I have prepared the way,' he said calmly. 'My name and my description have been added to the list of people with security clearance for emergencies. The people who *must* be let in to see the Prime Minister, if they give the right password for the day. And I have learnt today's password—*Disraeli*. All I have to do now is travel to Downing Street. So you can stop trying to think of a way to interfere with my plans. There is nothing you can do now.'

He glanced around the room, to make sure that all the Brains had heard him and understood. Then he began to turn away, to go back up to the front of the room.

But, while he was speaking, Dinah had glimpsed a movement, over his shoulder. A quiet, stealthy movement up at the front. The first time she saw it, she could hardly believe her eyes, but there it was.

At the front of the room, next to the S-700's main terminal and printer, was a rubbish chute with a flap across the opening. As Dinah watched, the flap was pushed up and a head emerged, followed by a body and a pair of legs. The figure crawled cautiously out, crept a little way across the room and ducked down behind the printer.

It was Lloyd.

Dinah had to use all her self-control to stop herself squealing with surprise. *I mustn't give him away*, she thought frantically. But what could she do? Already another head—Mandy's—was sticking out from under the flap. If the Headmaster turned round, he was sure to see the movements. And if he captured all the other members of SPLAT, that would be the end of everything.

Thinking quickly, Dinah reached out and grabbed at his sleeve, desperate to keep his attention on her.

'Look,' she said loudly, 'I don't just think your plans are wicked. I think they're stupid and inefficient. You've wasted all your energy planning this competition and setting up a gigantic computer program—and it will all be for nothing.'

'*What?*' Outraged, the Headmaster turned back to stare at her. 'You are talking nonsense.'

'No I'm not!' Dinah said. *Louder*, she thought. *I have to talk as loudly as I can, to drown any noises from the front.* She raised her voice until she was almost shouting and forced herself not to glance over his shoulder. 'You say you're going to take control of the Prime Minister's brain. And I'm sure you can do it. But what's the *point*? The Prime Minister's not all-powerful in this country.'

She could feel her voice giving out, beginning to croak with the strain of speaking so loudly and for a moment she wavered. Instantly, Bess picked up the argument. Had *she* seen the people crawling out of the rubbish chute as well?

'That's right!' she said, in a high, shrill tone. 'We're a *democracy*. The Prime Minister's not a dictator.'

Far away, at the front of the room, Ian and Ingrid and Harvey had all clambered out of the chute and hidden behind various cabinets. Somehow, without looking directly, Dinah was aware of them. And now she saw yet *another* head. Robert's! She was so pleased and relieved that she burst in as soon as Bess had finished, not waiting for the Headmaster to answer.

'*Please* change your mind. It's really not worth all the trouble, just for one measly Prime Minister and there must be lots of other ways to get power, if that's what you want. You could—'

'*Silence!*' The Headmaster was icy with anger. 'How dare you argue with me? You are only showing your own stupidity in failing to understand the full scope of my plans.'

'Tell us then!' yelled Bess.

'Yes!' shouted Dinah. *Tell us, and then you'll keep looking this way.*

'The Prime Minister is only a stepping stone,' the Headmaster said scornfully. 'Oh, I shan't have any trouble getting my own way with the Cabinet and the government. Not once I have been appointed the Prime Minister's valued adviser, present at all meetings.'

Present at all meetings. Dinah felt her face grow pale as she imagined it. The Headmaster looking round the Cabinet Room. Staring into the eyes of all the Cabinet Ministers and murmuring, 'You are feeling sleepy. Very, very sleepy . . . ' The Headmaster in the House of Commons itself, gazing up and down the long benches with his huge green eyes, until the clamour of MPs' voices grew still and there was silence over the whole Chamber. Oh, he could do it, she had no doubt of that. She shuddered.

'But that is only the beginning,' the Headmaster said triumphantly. 'Because the Prime Minister's trusted adviser will travel all over the world, of course. To summit meetings and international conferences. I shall be able to meet all the major world leaders face to face. Or *eyeball to eyeball*, as people say now.' He smiled thinly and Dinah realized, with a sort of horror, that he was so exultant that he had actually made a joke.

'But you mean you're actually going to hypnotize all the world leaders and take over everything that's mad you can't mean it,' Camilla said desperately. 'How can you think you know best about the whole world—?'

'Of *course* I know best,' the Headmaster said scornfully. 'And soon everyone will realize that I do. Nothing will be able to stop me once I have taken control of the Prime Minister's brain. And I shall have that within the next two hours.'

Ignoring Camilla's moan and Bess's white face and the gasps of the other Brains, he turned firmly away and began to stride up the room towards the main controls of the S-700. Everything at that end of the room was still now. Dinah was sure that, if she had not seen the figures creeping about and hiding behind the cabinets, she would never have guessed that they were there. Certainly the Headmaster did not guess. He was concentrating on the computer screen.

'We've got to stop him,' Camilla hissed across at

Bess and Dinah. 'It would be terrible if he succeeded but is he telling the truth can he really do it—?'

'You saw what he did to me,' Dinah muttered miserably. 'He doesn't fail with many people—and what could those few do against all the rest?'

'—but that would be like the end of the world we've got to stop him somehow but I can't see—'

'Well,' whispered Bess timidly, 'why don't we start with that security list he's put himself on? If he leaves us here when he goes off, we could take his name *off* again—and add in a warning to show them their security has been broken. After all, *we* know how to get into the Prime Minister's computer as well as he does.'

'You're right!' Dinah hissed. She gave Bess a friendly grin. 'We'll try that if we get a chance.'

The Headmaster could not have heard what they were saying, but when he had finished what he was doing, he looked up and spoke to the whole room.

'In a minute I shall leave you. But do not suppose that you will be able to interfere with my plans while I am gone. Or that you will be able to use the lift to escape from the building. To do either of those things, you would need to use the S-700—and I have set it on Automatic Booby Trap.'

For a moment, no one dared to speak. Then a nervous voice from the back of the room said, 'What's Automatic Booby Trap?'

The Headmaster smiled his thin, unpleasant smile. 'It is a wise precaution that I have built into the machine. Any attempt to use the S-700 now will short a special electric circuit and start a fire.' His smile grew even thinner and nastier. 'The fire will be in the lift, just to make sure that your escape is cut off. As you know, there are no stairs—no other way of getting down from here.'

'You mean,' the nervous voice said, 'that if we try to tamper with the S-700—we'll all die?'

The Headmaster nodded. 'It would be slow and very painful. And no one would be able to save you, because all my staff have now gone home and no one else will guess that you are here.'

'That's monstrous,' shouted Camilla, 'do you really mean to say that you would burn all these children to death just because—?'

'*No one* will burn to death,' said the Headmaster firmly, 'because no one will dare to interfere with my plans. It would be senseless. You will all simply stay here until I have time to make further arrangements for you. There is a good stock of food in the storerooms and the S-700 is programmed to provide you with regular meals in this room. You will all be perfectly safe. *As long as you obey my orders.*'

As he was speaking, Dinah became aware of a peculiar whirring noise outside the building. It grew louder and louder, closer and closer, coming up from the ground. As the Headmaster finished talking, it was directly above them. Then the voice of the S-700 sounded.

'Your Helicopter Is Overhead. Please Select Route Program And Open Roof Doors.'

'Goodbye,' said the Headmaster. 'Next time I see

you, we shall be living in a country that is being run *efficiently*. The beginning of a new, efficient world. All you have to do is wait. And I have given you something to help pass the time.'

He reached out and tapped at the S-700's keyboard. Immediately, the huge panels of the ceiling slid apart, letting in a blast of warm air. For the first time, Dinah realized that they were at the very top of the building, with nothing above them except blue sky. Hundreds of metres up in the air.

In the very centre of the patch of blue sky above them, a small single-seater helicopter was hovering. It was completely empty. As they watched, a rope ladder snaked down from the helicopter and through a gap in the roof. The Headmaster began to climb it, glancing over his shoulder from time to time to make sure that none of the Brains had moved.

He's getting away, Dinah thought unhappily. *And there's nothing we can do*.

As he reached the helicopter and started to pull the rope ladder up after him, the roof panels slid together again, smoothly and quietly. Dinah had a final view of the helicopter turning in the direction of central London. Then the sky was hidden and the Brains were alone in the room.

We must do something. But before Dinah could speak the words aloud, things began to happen.

The first was up at the front of the room. As soon as the Headmaster was safely out of the way, people darted out from behind the cabinets. Lloyd and Harvey. Ian and

Mandy and Ingrid. Robert. Even that other boy who had been taken away.

'Fantastic!' said Camilla. 'If Robert's OK we can stop worrying and start trying to make some kind of plan . . .'

But her voice died away, in the very middle of what she was saying. Her face went blank and she sat down suddenly, her eyes fixed on the screen on her desk.

All round the room, the same thing was happening. Lots of the Brains had jumped up in fear and rage as the Headmaster explained about the Automatic Booby Trap. Now they were all sitting down meekly. Watching the green lines that began to snake their way across every screen in the room.

Oct—

'No I won't!' Dinah said out loud, standing stubbornly beside her chair. She couldn't look. She had to explain everything to Lloyd and Robert and the others. Try to make some kind of plan—

Octo—

But all round her, on every side, green lines wriggled and arched and danced . . .

Octopus—

'No!' she said again. But this time she did not manage to sound so determined. After all, Lloyd and the others were already running down the room towards her. What harm could there be in just glancing at the lovely intricate curling lines that spiralled and sparkled and spun and . . .

Octopus - s - s - s - s!

17

THE BRAINS FIGHT BACK

'*No!*'

Lloyd heard Dinah's shriek when he was halfway down the room. Before he had time to wonder what she meant, there was another shriek behind him, from Ingrid.

'Oh no! Not more octopuses!'

Octopuses! At the mere sound of the word, Lloyd felt himself filling with dark, speechless rage. So the Headmaster was doing it again, was he? Thinking he could treat people just like machines. Press the right button and they'll do what you want. Show them a few octopus patterns and they won't be any trouble. Well, he wasn't going to be treated like that! He screwed his eyes up so tightly that he could not see anything except prickles of light against the blackness of his eyelids.

'Ian!' he shouted. 'Mandy! Robert and Doug! Shut your eyes quickly and *don't open them*!' Then he thought fast. 'Ing, are you and Harvey all right?'

'*We're* OK,' Ingrid said scornfully. 'But we seem to be the only ones. The whole room's full of people gawping at octopuses. Pathetic!'

'Well, is there some way we can switch off the

screens?' Lloyd turned towards Robert. 'Could you tell Ingrid how to turn the computer off?'

'Not safe,' Robert said firmly. 'You heard what the Computer Director said before he left. Any interference with the computer will start a fire.'

'But there must be *something* we can do.' Lloyd thought even harder. 'Can we cover up the main screen? Is there any paper?'

'Gallons.' All of a sudden, Robert sounded much brisker and more cheerful. 'There's loads of paper in the printer up the front. If Ingrid and Harvey stuck that all over the main screen, to hide the octopuses, then they could unplug all the monitors on the desks. That ought to be safe. It's not really interfering with the main computer.'

'Right,' said Lloyd. 'Hear that, Ingrid and Harvey? That's what you'll have to do. Cover the main screen first and then turn off the monitors. Got that? Ingrid! Harvey! What are you doing?'

'Don't be thick!' Ingrid's voice came from far up at the front. 'We didn't wait for you to tell us. We started as soon as Robert had the idea. We've nearly finished the main screen already.'

Lloyd bit back the cross answer that came to his lips. After all, if he annoyed Ingrid, they were all in trouble. Next to him he heard Ian chuckle.

'Horrible being dependent on those two, isn't it?' he drawled. 'Ingrid will really enjoy having us under her thumb.'

'Oh, Ian, don't be *mean*!' Mandy said, on Lloyd's

other side. 'We're jolly lucky that Ingrid and Harvey *aren't* addicted to the octopus patterns. If they had sat and watched them, like everyone else at the Computer Club, we'd all be fumbling around with our eyes shut now.'

'No we wouldn't,' Lloyd said bitterly. 'We'd all be standing like dummies in the Restraint Room. Like we were until Ingrid switched off *that* screen.'

As he finished speaking, Ingrid called from the front of the room. 'That's done! Now we'll do the monitors. Won't be long. Come on, Harvey.'

There was a sound of feet pattering down the room, stopping at every desk and then pattering on again at top speed. Mandy sighed anxiously.

'It's so awful not being able to *see*. Do you think I should take a peep? Just so we know how they're getting on?'

'No!' Lloyd's answer was fierce. But he knew what she meant. He was aching to open his own eyes. Just to get one more sight of those lovely swirling octopus patterns that he was missing. Those beautiful, twining . . .

No!

They had to defeat the Headmaster. *Somehow*. Otherwise he would take over the country and then the world. Nothing else mattered beside stopping that. Gritting his teeth, Lloyd screwed his eyes up even tighter and growled at the others. 'Don't you *dare* look until Ingrid and Harvey say we can.'

It seemed like another six or seven hours, but it

could only have been a couple of minutes before Harvey called, 'It's all safe now. You can open your eyes.'

Lloyd unscrewed his, blinking in the brightness of the room. There was not an octopus to be seen. All round him, the monitors were blank and when he glanced over his shoulder he saw the thick cover of paper that Ingrid and Harvey had sellotaped over the main screen. They had made a good job of it.

On every side, Brains were rubbing their eyes and glancing round. Lloyd could tell from their horrified faces that they were just beginning to remember the frightful trap they were in. Some of the little ones had started to cry softly and the older ones were pale and tense. For a second, no one spoke and then a tall girl with long hair launched herself at Robert from the middle of the room.

'Oh Robert Robert thank goodness you're safe I've been so worried about you but did you hear the terrible things the Computer Director said how are we going to stop him—*what are we going to do?*'

As if she had pressed a switch, every head in the room turned in their direction. Big and small, old and young, all the Brains were staring at Robert and Lloyd as though they expected them to produce some marvellous plan. And the girl's question hung in the air, ringing in everyone's ear.

What are we going to do?

They had been freed from the octopuses, but the Headmaster was still flying across London in his helicopter, on his way to take over the Prime Minister's brain. And any attempt to use the computer to stop him or to escape from the building would start a fire. For a moment, Lloyd wondered whether they wouldn't all have been better off looking at the octopuses.

Then Dinah appeared beside him, so quietly that he did not notice her coming. She did not waste time saying how surprised she was to see him or asking how he got there. She just gave him a small, grateful smile and then turned to face the rest of the Brains, looking as calm as ever.

'Listen, everyone,' she said, in a steady, controlled voice, 'you don't need me to tell you what the choice is. You're all clever enough to work it out for yourselves. We can't escape from the building because we would need to use the computer to work the lift. So—we've got to decide. Are we going to sit back and wait for the country to be taken over? Or are we going to try and use the computer to warn the Downing Street security staff—even if it means burning to death?'

For a moment there was silence. Then a small girl, who was clutching a teddy bear, said timidly, 'I think we've *got* to do something. We can't just let him get away with it. It would be like the world coming to an end for everyone.' She stopped and swallowed hard before she added, 'Instead of just for us.'

'Right then, everyone,' Dinah said, in her inexpressive voice. 'We'd better vote. Who agrees with Bess that we should stop this evil plan—whatever happens to us afterwards?'

As she finished speaking, she put up her own hand,

her thin arm looking very straight and steady. And one by one, all over the room, the other hands went up as the Brains voted with her. Some of them were crying and some of them looked frightened and sick, but they all voted to fight back against the Headmaster.

'What about you?' Dinah turned to the members of SPLAT. 'You ought to have a vote too.'

Lloyd had actually put his hand halfway up before his mind began to work properly. He had been so full of admiration for the Brains' bravery that he had not been *thinking*. Now he suddenly exploded.

'But we're *stupid*! *I'm stupid*. No one needs to burn to death!' He could see them all staring at him, and he hurried to explain, the words tumbling over themselves. 'Listen—the fire will start in the lift. Right? At the back of the room. Well, we can all escape down the rubbish chute, the way the five of us came up. We've got ropes and most of us can get away before anyone *touches* the computer if we're quick. You don't need many people to stay and work it, do you?'

Dinah shook her head. 'I could do it. With one other person to watch me in case I made a mistake.' Her eyes were suddenly very bright.

'Well, I think you could escape as well,' Lloyd said. 'The rubbish chute will be on the opposite side of the building to the fire. If you're quick and you climb down fast you should have time.'

'Fantastic brilliant oh how marvellous to have something we can *do* I'll help to organize everyone to climb down where are the ropes—'

That was Robert's sister. But she was not just babbling. Even while she was talking, she had begun to organize the front rows of Brains to march towards the rubbish chute. And she had got Ian and Mandy knotting the ropes together to form a long string that would stretch all the way down the chute. Robert grinned at Lloyd.

'Don't let Camilla put you off. She only *sounds* thick. She'll get everyone out of here faster than anyone else could. And I'll stay and help Dinah change the information on the computer if she explains what she's doing. The rest of you can leave us here.'

'Not me,' Lloyd said. 'I can't go until I know we've stopped the Headmaster. But the others can.'

Ingrid tossed her head. 'Me and Harvey are staying. You might *need* us. Suppose you come across some more octopuses.'

Lloyd hesitated for a moment. Then he nodded. She was being sensible for once. 'OK. But that makes five of us left up here. We can't risk any more. Harvey, go and tell Ian and Mandy to go down with the others and leave the ropes for us.'

The room was already starting to look empty. A lot of the Brains were on their way down the rubbish chute and those who were left were crowded round the entrance, waiting for their turn to squeeze under the flap. Dinah and Robert were huddled together at one of the desks, bent over a piece of paper, working out what they were going to do with the computer. Everyone was moving at a feverish pace. Lloyd shuddered slightly and hoped that it was not too late already. He did not know how long it would take a small helicopter to fly to the centre of London—but it could not be long.

Dinah glanced up as the last Brain wriggled under the flap. 'OK. I think we ought to start now. I'll do the first bit without switching on the screen, until I've got rid of the octopuses.'

Stretching out a finger, she pressed a key on the keyboard in front of her.

Immediately, the mechanical robot-voice rang through the empty room, startling them all.

'This Computer Is Booby-Trapped. Any Further Tampering Will Set Fire To The Building.'

'I think he meant it,' Robert murmured softly. 'Let's just hope it doesn't take too long.'

Without bothering to speak, Dinah nodded again and pressed another key and another. Lloyd looked nervously towards the lift doors. But nothing dramatic happened. There was no explosion, no instant burst of flame. What was it that the Headmaster had said? That it would be *slow and very painful*. Lloyd shuddered. Then his attention was drawn back to the computer. Dinah switched on the monitor.

'Let's just see what's running at the moment.'

For a second they all thought she had blundered, because what was on the screen was an octopus. But it was different from the usual twisting, swirling octopuses. This one was very still with all its tentacles stretched out straight, crossing the screen diagonally and pointing at a tiny blob in the top right-hand corner.

Behind the octopus, covering the screen like a sort of backcloth and moving all the time, as if it were unrolling, was a street map of London.

'What on earth—?' said Robert.

Lloyd and Dinah looked just as baffled, but Ingrid gave a loud squawk.

'Harvey—look! Oh, Lloyd, you'll never guess what—'

But before she could finish her sentence, Lloyd smelt what he had been afraid of all the time. Scorching. Turning his head, he saw a small wisp of smoke curling under the lift doors.

'Be quiet, Ingrid!' he snapped. 'There's no time for chattering. Hurry up, Dinah.'

'But if you'd only *listen* —' protested Ingrid.

'Ssh!' hissed Lloyd. Really, she was hopeless. She had no idea of how desperate things were.

'But, Lloyd,' Harvey joined in, 'if you'd only let us *tell* you—'

Lloyd nearly shouted at him. 'Don't you understand? *The lift is on fire.* If Robert and Dinah aren't very quick, we'll all burn to death. So don't distract them.'

Harvey looked unhappy and Ingrid sniffed and turned away, but they both stopped talking. Lloyd looked back at the screen and as he did so, Robert said, 'Found it! Well done, Dinah. Now you can get going.'

Across the screen spread a single sentence.

WHAT DO YOU WANT?

Dinah tapped at the keys, typing in a reply, and for a moment Lloyd thought she had gone mad as the lines of print—question and answer—began to fill the screen.

KNOCK KNOCK
WHO'S THERE
OLGA
OLGA WHO?

Robert caught sight of his face and grinned. 'Password,' he murmured. 'Look, she's putting in the last line now.'

OLGA MAD IF I DON'T GET OFF THIS LOOP

Sure enough, as Dinah typed it in the joke vanished and a long catalogue appeared on the screen heading:

PRIME MINISTER

PERSONAL INFORMATION

'That's what it was all about,' Robert said softly. 'The Junior Computer Brain Competition and *Octopus Dare* and everyone being invited here. All so that your Headmaster could get at *that*.'

'Well, now *I'm* going to get at it,' Dinah said. She pressed the right key to select the list of:

PEOPLE TO BE ADMITTED TO PRIME MINISTER TOP PRIORITY.

It was a fairly long list and she searched through it at feverish speed. Lloyd knew why she was hurrying so hard. A mist of smoke had drifted up in front of the lift doors and was slowly working its way down the room.

'There!' Dinah said at last. 'I've taken the Headmaster's name out. And I've replaced it with a warning—so that they know security has been breached when they look for him. That *should* fix him.'

'You mean you've done it?' Lloyd felt like cheering. 'We've defeated his plans?'

Dinah nodded. 'We've done everything we can.' But she did not look very happy. Lloyd peered at her, trying to ignore the crackling sounds that were coming from the lift.

'What's the matter, Di?'

'We-ell.' Dinah pulled a face. 'We've done all we can, but—suppose it's not enough? Suppose they don't bother to check the security list? The Headmaster's gone off to Number Ten Downing Street with today's password in his head and there's no way we can wipe *that* out. They might just let him in when he gives the right password. And then . . . ' She let her voice die away and shrugged. 'Oh well, we'll just have to hope for the best. Like I said, there's nothing else we can do.'

She had stood up and was turning towards the rubbish chute when Ingrid suddenly exploded in a great yell.

'YES THERE IS, YOU STUPID IDIOTS!' she shouted. 'THERE *IS* SOMETHING ELSE WE CAN DO!!'

18

THE LAST OCTOPUS

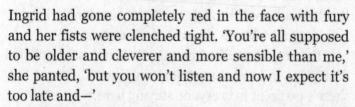

Ingrid had gone completely red in the face with fury
and her fists were clenched tight. 'You're all supposed
to be older and cleverer and more sensible than me,'
she panted, 'but you won't listen and now I expect it's
too late and—'

'Ingrid!' Dinah caught her by the shoulders. 'If
there's anything you can tell us—*anything*—then tell
us. But please do it now, because there's almost no time
left.'

They could all smell the scorching now, very strongly,
and the doors of the lift were beginning to darken in the
centre, as though the flames were eating a hole in them.

'It's—it's—' But Ingrid's rage had made her so
breathless that she could not speak. She faced Dinah
and struggled to gulp in enough air to say what she
wanted to, but no sound came out.

'*I'll* tell you what she wants to say,' Harvey
interrupted. 'We've been trying to tell people ever since
we got into this tower. We saw that helicopter in the car
park and it had an octopus picture on its control panel.
Just like that octopus picture we saw on the screen just
now, with the map of London behind it and—'

But Robert had already worked it out, in a flash.

'And we know that the S-700 controls the helicopter, so perhaps *that* octopus picture is a diagram of how it does it. And perhaps *we* could get control of the helicopter and turn it back.'

Dinah looked at him very steadily for a second, her face white. Then she glanced across at the lift doors. As she did so, a small hole appeared in the centre of it. Flames licked through the hole, shockingly bright, reaching out towards the rest of the room.

'The rest of you had better go,' Dinah said quietly. 'I'm going to have a go at stopping the helicopter, but there's no point in everyone staying here.'

'Go on.' Lloyd jerked his head at the other three. 'I'm staying with Dinah.'

For a moment it looked as though Robert would argue, but instead he shepherded Ingrid and Harvey towards the rubbish chute as Dinah sat down in front of the computer again.

Lloyd looked nervously over his shoulder. He had no intention of letting Dinah stay on her own, but he hoped she would *hurry*. The far end of the room was completely filled with smoke now and the doorway of the lift was a bright square of flame.

'There we are,' Dinah said softly. 'There's the picture again.'

She made herself sit very still for a second, just studying it, gripping her two hands together to stop them trembling. It was no use being afraid. She had to concentrate on what she was doing.

As soon as she looked at the picture properly, she

could see that Ingrid and Harvey were right. It was a diagram of how the S-700 controlled the helicopter. The octopus's body represented the S-700 and the tentacles were the lines of force going out to the helicopter—like radio waves going out to a remote-controlled model plane. The map in the background showed where the helicopter was, above the ground. And it was—Dinah peered at the map and then gulped—it was almost above Downing Street. She had only about a minute left. Perhaps no more than thirty seconds.

Her fingers closed round the mouse and she began to move it, cautiously at first and then faster and faster. Immediately she began, the octopus's tentacles started to move, answering the movements of the mouse. And as the tentacles moved, so did the blob which represented the helicopter. Instead of travelling in a steady straight line across the map, it began to whirl and dance.

'It's like a sort of *Reverse Octopus Dare*,' murmured Lloyd. 'This time you're the octopus instead of the blob. And *you've* got the helicopter at *your* mercy.'

'Not properly at my mercy,' Dinah said, sounding flustered. She was struggling to make the tentacles turn the helicopter round and bring it back, but somehow she could not quite get a grip on it. And all the time she was aware of smoke billowing closer, starting to sting her eyes. 'I can flick the blob—the helicopter—about, but I can't get hold of it properly.'

'Well, flick it *down*,' Lloyd said fiercely. He could feel the warmth of the fire against his back. 'Make him crash. We haven't got time to hang about.'

'All right,' said Dinah. She reached out to do what he had suggested. And then it hit her. *Make him crash. Him.* It was not a game like *Octopus Dare* that she was playing. And the blob she had been playing with was not a blob. It was a helicopter. With a person inside. Feeling sick, she took her hand off the mouse and pushed her chair backwards.

'What's the matter?' Lloyd almost screamed it at her. 'Di, we've got to *go*. You must finish it now.'

'I can't do it,' Dinah said stiffly. 'I'm sorry, but even if it is the Headmaster—*I can't kill him.*'

'Oh, for heaven's sake!' Lloyd shouted. 'If you dither any longer, he'll get to the Prime Minister and we'll burn to death.'

He reached over her shoulder, meaning to do it himself. It was as easy as playing a computer game. But as soon as he got within touching distance of the mouse, he faltered and stopped.

'You see?' Dinah said miserably. '*You* can't, either. And anyway, think how dangerous it would be, crashing a helicopter in the middle of London.'

Lloyd coughed as the smoke caught the back of his throat. 'If only we could just get him *away*.'

'We can!' In a flash, Dinah saw it, with a great burst of relief. 'I won't flick him down—I'll flick him *up*, as far as I can. Right away. Then we must race down the rope, before it's too late. Ready?'

With her eyes watering so that she could hardly see and her ears full of the roaring of the flames, she reached for the mouse.

Outside the entrance to Downing Street, a crowd of people had gathered to watch the strange sight up in the evening sky.

A small helicopter was tumbling head over heels, twirling round in a most extraordinary way. Was the pilot drunk? Had he gone mad?

The helicopter swooped down towards the earth. For a moment, the watchers had a glimpse of a cold, furious face. A face with huge, strange, sea-green eyes. It glared down at the crowd, the amazing eyes burning with unforgettable rage.

Then, just as suddenly as it had swooped, the helicopter soared upwards, as though someone had flicked it up and thrown it. Up and up, further and further into the brilliance of the sunset, with the light glinting from its spotless glass dome.

Then it whirled away to the west and disappeared in the far distance.

Five minutes later, Lloyd jumped down from the dustbin and raced out of the underground car park, dragging Dinah after him. Smoke filled the air outside and they did not stop to see what was happening. They plunged straight across to the subway that led off North Island and raced down the steps.

So it was not until they came out beside the station that they looked back. They came up the steps and found all the Brains gathered in a huge crowd, gazing back across the motorway intersection. Ingrid and Harvey and Mandy were in the very front of the crowd and they pointed silently, until Lloyd and Dinah turned to see.

The Sentinel Tower was a huge pillar of flame, one hundred metres high. Even from where they were standing, they could feel the heat of the flames and hear the noise of splintering glass and falling metal. The outer framework, which held the giant mirror panes, was glowing red hot as the mirrors shattered and showered to the ground.

For a moment Dinah could only think what a stunning sight it was. Then something occurred to her and a slow, relieved smile spread over her face.

'It really *is* the end of the Headmaster's plan,' she said softly. 'His whole scheme for running the country was stored on the S-700. In that building. Now it's gone.'

She heard a tiny snuffle at her elbow. Looking round, she saw Ingrid wipe her eyes.

'Whatever's the matter, Ing? You can't be sorry.'

'I'm *not* crying!' Ingrid said fiercely.

'No, of course you're not. But—'

'It's that lovely computer,' Ingrid burst out. 'That S-700. All burnt up.'

'But, *Ingrid*!' Lloyd and Harvey and Ian and Mandy all said it together, turning to stare at her. 'You *hate* computers!'

'Not that one,' Ingrid said pathetically. 'How can

you hate a computer when you've seen it cooking the dinner and treating Harvey like a packet of spaghetti? It was a lovely computer. *Funny.* And it could talk. I bet I could have got it to say *Down With The Headmaster!*'

Mandy put an arm round her. 'Never mind. Don't you remember all those SPLAT things we were going to do this holidays? The picnic and the camp and the visit to the Science Museum? We could still fit in a couple of them before the beginning of term.'

'Oh yes. Of course,' said Ingrid. But she did not look any more cheerful.

'And you can forget all about computers!' added Harvey.

'But computers are *fun*!' wailed Ingrid. She looked ready to burst into tears properly.

Lloyd and Dinah looked at each other.

'Do you think we could tell her now?' Lloyd murmured.

'I *think* so.' Dinah grinned. 'I think it would be safe.'

'What?' Ingrid looked up sharply. 'What are you two talking about?'

Lloyd chuckled. 'Mr Meredith says we're getting loads of new computers at school next term.'

Ingrid glanced at Dinah, as though she could hardly believe it, and Dinah nodded. 'That's right. And I'll show you how to do things with them. We might not manage cooking, but it'll be simple to get them to say *Down with the Headmaster!*'

'WHOOPEE!' Ingrid's high, delighted shout

screeched up into the night sky, making all the Brains laugh.

There was so much noise that only Lloyd and Dinah heard what Ian murmured as he glanced back at the blazing Sentinel Tower.

'I wonder where he *did* come down . . .'

PREPARE TO FALL UNDER THE DEMON
HEADMASTER'S SPELL ONCE MORE.

READ ON FOR A TASTE OF . . .

It was six o'clock before they got to Ingrid's. Dinah tried to slip off home, but Lloyd wouldn't let her.

'This is a SPLAT meeting, and that means we stick together. You've *got* to come.'

Dinah didn't look pleased, but she went to Ingrid's and sat down in the front room, with the rest of them.

'It won't take long,' Ingrid said, as she switched on the television. 'Not if we're only going to watch one programme. Are you sure — ?'

'Sure,' Lloyd said firmly.

'Then I'll show you the first one Auntie Rachel let me watch. I was still quite ill then. But the moment I saw it I was hooked.'

She found the programme and sat back, with a pleased expression on her face. Almost immediately, the screen was filled by a huge, slobbery pig's face, exactly the same as the one on the front of her T-shirt. It cocked its head and spoke smugly.

'*Who's always right?*'

A hundred voices roared the answer, as the words splashed across the screen.

'HUNKY PARKER!!!'

The pig blew a raspberry, drooling bubbles from its snout. Then it waddled away from the camera, into a neat, clean kitchen, where the table was laid for breakfast.

'I just love eating with the family,' it said. 'I'm an ED-u-cated pig!'

Seizing a packet of cornflakes, it began to tip them into its mouth, showering crumbs all over the table.

Lloyd stared. Ingrid thought *this* was brilliant? Had she gone mad? He didn't know if he could sit through a quarter of an hour of it.

He looked round at the others. Dinah had already given up. She'd slipped the maths book out of her pocket and was reading that, totally ignoring the rogramme. Lloyd shook his head. He ought to *make* her watch. But how could he, when it was such rubbish?

Glancing back at the screen, he saw Hunky Parker pick up a tin of golden syrup and empty it on to the table, on top of the sugar and toast and cornflakes he'd already spilt. *Bor-ing*, Lloyd thought.

And then something very odd happened.

While Hunky Parker was spilling the golden syrup, he just looked horrible. Fat and smug and grubby. But, as he threw the tin on to the floor, something changed.

Not Hunky Parker himself. He was just as fat and smug and grubby as before. The change was in Lloyd's mind. Suddenly, that fatness and smugness and grubbiness wasn't horrible any more. Hunky Parker looked at the camera, grinned a dribbling grin and said, '*Who's always right?*'—and Lloyd found himself laughing.

He would have felt silly, but Mandy and Ian and Harvey were laughing too. And Ingrid was clutching her sides and rolling around on the couch. Only Dinah was quiet, buried in her book. How *could* she? When Hunky Parker was so . . . so . . .

Ready for more great stories?

CAN YOU RESIST . . . ?